EIGHT TALES
FOR EIGHT NIGHTS

The illustrations for these tales were created by Tsirl Waletzky in paper-cut, a traditional art form deeply rooted in Jewish practice and folklore. The Judaic paper-cut can be traced back at least to the seventeenth century, in the various centers of Jewish communal life. It often reflected the surrounding cultures, adding to the richness of its own visual symbolic language. Kin to illumination, the Judaic paper-cut was, and is, used for *ketubot* (marriage contracts), *mizrahs* (decorative parchments placed on the eastern wall of a house to indicate the direction in which Jerusalem lies), amulets, holiday decorations, illustrations, and more. It is a vibrant and ever-expanding area of Jewish art expression.

EIGHT TALES FOR EIGHT NIGHTS

Stories for Chanukah

Peninnah Schram
and
Steven M. Rosman

Illustrations by Tsirl Waletzky

Jason Aronson Inc.
Northvale, New Jersey
London

To All My Readers: I hope these tales I bring light and laughter to you.

Steven M. Rosman

Library of Congress Cataloging-in-Publication Data

Schram, Peninnah.
    Eight tales for eight nights : stories for Chanukah / Peninnah Schram and Steven M. Rosman : illustrations by Tsirl Waletzky.
       p. cm.
    Summary: Eight traditional tales from around the world introduce the customs and meanings of Chanukah.
    ISBN 0-87668-749-4 (hardcover)
    ISBN 0-87668-234-4 (softcover)
    1. Hanukkah. [1. Hanukkah. 2. Folklore, Jewish.]   I. Rosman, Steven M. II. Waletzky, Tsirl, ill.   III. Title. IV. Title: 8 tales for 8 nights.
BM695.H3S39   1990   90-39599
                                                    CIP
                                                        AC

Manufactured in the United States of America. Jason Aronson Inc. offers books and cassettes. For information and catalog write to Jason Aronson Inc., 230 Livingston Street, Northvale, New Jersey 07647.

To my husband, Jerry Thaler, and to our children, Susan and Daniel, Naomi and Barry, Magda and Jonathan, Rebecca and Emile, and Michael, and to our grandchildren, Rebecca and Ruby, Noah and Mark, and Max, who have continually helped me discover new stories of miracles and light!

P.S.

To my wife, Bari, whose love and constant support have enabled me to grow and to discover the person I wish to become, and to my daughter, Michal, whose very life and being have blessed me with renewed optimism and recognition of life's simplest and most profound treasures.

S.M.R.

Contents

Preface xi

Acknowledgment xv

How Chanukah Came to Be
1

The First Night
The Picture in the Flame
An Eastern European Tale
11

The Second Night
The Secret of the Shammash
A Sephardi Tale
25

The Third Night
Chanukah Means Hope
A Holocaust Tale
37

The Fourth Night
A Secret Chanukah
A Marrano Tale
49

The Fifth Night
How to Sell a Menorah!
An Eastern European Tale
59

The Sixth Night
A Stranger's Gift
A Persian Tale
69

The Seventh Night
The Rescued Menorah
An American Tale
79

The Eighth Night
A Melody in Israel
An Israeli Tale
91

Appendix 1   Music for Chanukah Blessings
              and *Hanerot Halalu*   119

Appendix 2   Retrieving Family Stories   127

Appendix 3   The Second Shammash:
              Two Chanukah Memories   139

Appendix 4   Story and Music Sources   149

Glossary   155

Preface

Eight Tales for Eight Nights: Stories for Chanukah is an intergenerational holiday book. These eight stories, written in the oral tradition, are meant to be told or read aloud. They are intended to teach the customs and meanings of Chanukah as practiced throughout the ages in countries where Jews have lived, and to inspire the readers to create their own stories. Our hope is that these eight stories will spark the reader's imagination.

Chanukah is a post-biblical holiday of lights, charity, gift-giving, food, games, song, and story. Of course, the story of the holiday itself, found in the Apocryphal Books of Maccabees I and II, is the most important. The retelling of this story continues to re-create the celebration of our freedom as a Jewish people.

We have designed what amounts to a literary *chanu-*

kiah. Just as the *shammash* kindles each of the other eight candles, so our retelling of the traditional rabbinic legend "How Chanukah Came to Be" is the touchstone for eight subsequent tales that explore a wealth of themes such as freedom, thanksgiving, dedication, the miracle of lights, Jewish heroes and heroines, Jewish pride, and miracles. As each night arrives, and with it the kindling of another taper, the family looks forward to sharing another tale. At such a holiday, when so much is happening in the home—the ritual of lighting the candles and reciting the blessings, eating special foods as a way of connecting to the story, welcoming relatives and friends, playing dreidle, singing songs, and retelling the story of the holiday— it is an especially appropriate time to share more stories.

All the tales in this book are rooted in those themes found in the traditional Chanukah legend that serves as our *shammash*. These tales take place in regions in the world where Jews have lived: Eastern Europe, Asia, the Middle East, America, Israel. Both the Ashkenazi and Sephardi-Oriental traditions are represented. The tales take place in various times: in the sixth, fifteenth, eighteenth, and nineteenth centuries, during the Holocaust, after World War II, in the late 1940s when Israel became a State, and today. The moods found in the stories range from poignant to humorous. There are love stories, a trickster story, an etiological story—all filled with magic and miracles. Elijah the Prophet, the most beloved hero in Jewish folklore, the famous jester Hershele Ostropolier, grandmothers and grandfathers, mysterious strangers, rabbis, children, and a king are found in these stories. Music is integral to two of them, "The Picture in the Flame" and "A Melody in Israel." We have placed the actual music at the end of each of these stories, as an option for the reader/storyteller to use, rather than interweaving the musical notes throughout the text itself. The stories can be told without the songs, although the songs will add a great deal.

While the stories form the core of this book, they are not its sole content. There are also a glossary, which describes or defines the Yiddish and Hebrew words and terms used in the stories, and appendixes. The first appendix is comprised of music for the Chanukah blessings, the song *Hanerot Halalu* in both Ashkenazi and Western Sephardi versions, and an original composition. The second appendix discusses the Jewish oral tradition, and suggests how you the reader can retrieve and reclaim your own personal experience and family stories for the holiday. We believe that adding your own stories to the traditional tales can create a strong and special bond between the generations. These stories will become a treasured legacy. In the third appendix we offer two Chanukah-memory stories that we have reclaimed from our own histories. They are meant to serve as sparks to inspire you to search within yourself for your own memory stories. The fourth appendix is a bibliography of music and story sources.

When we were working on the idea of this book, and actually writing it, we hoped that our readers would use the book during the Chanukah Festival, after the lighting of the candles each night, in the following ways:

    1. On the first night of Chanukah, read or tell the story of Chanukah as we have retold it here. Then read one of the stories in the book.

2. On the second night of Chanukah, have your children (or other members of the family or friends) repeat the story of Chanukah that they have been told. Then read a second story from the book.

3. Each night, read one of the stories from the book. In addition, have someone in the group tell a personal or family memory or vignette about Chanukah, using some of the suggested exercises in Appendixes 2 and 3.

Our hopes, then, are that the stories in this book will be shared—by grandparents and grandchildren, by mothers and fathers with sons and daughters, by older children with younger children, by teachers and students, by all storytellers with their listeners as they celebrate the holiday together, this holiday of light and miracle and story.

Acknowledgment

We gratefully acknowledge the support of our friend, Arthur Kurzweil, vice president of Jason Aronson, whose love of story and storytelling encouraged us to write these tales. We express our appreciation to the entire Jason Aronson production staff for their expertise and diligence in producing this book, especially production editor Jane Andrassi and copy editor Nancy Berliner. We thank our artist, Tsirl Waletzky, for her enthusiasm and extraordinary talents in creating the splendid paper-cuts that wonderfully illustrate the stories. We also want to thank Cantor Marla Barugel, Dr. Albert Barugel, and Velvel Pasternak, who served as music consultants. And a special thanks to our spouses, Jerry Thaler and Bari Ziegel, for their readings of the stories through the various drafts and their insightful suggestions.

How Chanukah Came to Be

Tsirl Waletzky

More than two thousand years ago, there lived a powerful but wicked king of Syria whose name was Antiochus. Antiochus ruled an enormous empire of many different lands. One of these countries was the entire land of Israel. There is a saying that "the ways of the wicked are like deep darkness," and this was certainly true of Antiochus, for he was so mean and cruel that he made it a very dark time, a scary time, and a sad time for everyone who lived in his kingdom.

Antiochus thought he was a god, so he ordered statues of himself to be placed in every town in the land. He wanted people to bow down to his statue and worship him with all the other Greek gods. If the people refused, he would order his soldiers to take their swords and kill

5

them right there on the spot. The only religion that was allowed now was the religion of Antiochus.

Imagine—there could be no more Jewish holidays, no more Jewish celebrations, no more Jewish Temple in Jerusalem. As his first order, Antiochus commanded that the great Temple be destroyed. He ordered his soldiers to tear it apart, to burn the Torah scrolls, to destroy the holy Ark, and in its place, to erect a statue of Antiochus.

One day, Antiochus's soldiers came to a small town called Modin. Modin was not far from Jerusalem and many faithful Jews lived there. The soldiers rode big black horses and brought gigantic carts with them. In the carts were statues of Antiochus. The soldiers lifted the statues out of the carts and began to place them all around town. The people of Modin gathered around the carts to see what the soldiers were doing. The captain of the guards announced to them: "Antiochus orders all the people in Modin to assemble tomorrow morning in the center of the town. You will bring gifts to the god Antiochus and bow down to his statues. You will kiss the feet of his statues and take and oath to worship him."

When the Jews in Modin heard this, they became worried. "What shall we do?" they cried. "We are Jews! We have only one God: the God of Abraham, Isaac, and Jacob, the God who gave us the Torah. We cannot worship other gods. But if we refuse, the soldiers will kill us."

The next day, everyone in Modin came to the center of town. The soldiers were there sharpening their swords. The captain called out his orders: "Everyone line up! Line up before your new god, Antiochus!"

6

The Jews did as they were told.

"You there," called out the captain. "You are the first in line. Come up here and kiss the feet of the god Antiochus."

Slowly, the first person in line came forward. But just as he did, a man ran in front of him and blocked his way. It was Mattathias, one of God's priests.

"No Jew will ever bow down to an idol," Mattathias declared. "Our God is not Antiochus. We have only one God, and we will not let you take away our holidays, our Temple, and our rituals."

Mattathias stood right in front of the captain as he spoke. His words made the captain turn red with anger and shake with rage. The captain seized his sword to slay Mattathias, but Mattathias swiftly pulled a knife from under his robe and stabbed the captain first.

"Let all who want to fight the evil Antiochus follow me!" shouted Mattathias as he ran through the town. And before Antiochus's guards knew what was happening, Mattathias had escaped with his sons and other Jews.

Antiochus was enraged when he heard what had happened in Modin. "Who does this Mattathias think he is?" he barked. "Does he think he can defy me? I will teach him never to disobey me again."

So Antiochus sent a troop of soldiers to find Mattathias and throw him in prison. But Mattathias was hard to find. He and his followers were hiding in the caves of the Judean hillside, which they knew so well. Their small group was led by one of Mattathias's five sons, Judah, who was a very clever leader. Whenever Antiochus's soldiers passed by, Judah and his men would leap from their hiding place and jump on the soldiers and shout,

"There is no God like our God!" With all their heavy armor, shields, and spears, the soldiers could only move very slowly, and by the time they recovered from the surprise attack, Judah and his men had disappeared back into the hills.

As word spread of Judah and his group, they came to be known as the Maccabees, meaning "hammers," because they pounced on their enemies like a hammer hits a nail. Then, before their foes knew what had hit them, Judah and his band were gone.

Antiochus tried many times to defeat the Maccabees, but each time Judah outsmarted him and won the battle. Finally, Antiochus knew he was defeated. He had lost too many good soldiers. So Antiochus took what remained of his armies away from the land of Judea. The Maccabees had won!

Though Antiochus was gone, the signs of his fury remained. He had destroyed so many things in Judea. He had ruined many Jewish towns. He had put up his statues everywhere. He had defiled the holy Temple in Jerusalem.

Judah Maccabee and his men wept when they saw what had been done to the holy Temple. There was garbage everywhere. Pigs and other animals had been sacrificed on the altar. The beautiful curtains around the Ark had been ripped and slashed. The Torah scrolls lay torn and burned. The *Ner Tamid* had been extinguished. And in the middle of the sanctuary lay the Temple's magnificent *menorah*, overturned with all the oil spilled from its cups.

Judah Maccabee suddenly sounded a series of blasts on his trumpet. "Ta, ta! Ta, ta! Ta, ta!"

"Look what I have found," called Judah. In his hand was a small jar. "It is oil," he said. "The pure oil that our priests used to light the great *menorah*. There is not very much inside, but we will use what we have."

He moved to the *menorah* and set it upright. Carefully, he poured the oil into one of its cups and lit the wick.

A beautiful flame arose. It flickered, and then it glowed. The Maccabees were inspired by the sight of the flame burning in the *menorah* again.

"God is here with us," said Judah. "This is God's flame, and this Temple is God's house. Let us make it fit for God to visit again."

Judah and his men worked very hard to clean up the Temple. They polished the silver cups and candlesticks. They pulled the weeds from the earthen floor. They washed the walls and the floors, and they mended the curtains and rebuilt the Ark. This took them many days, and all the while, as they worked to clean the Temple, the flame in the *menorah* continued to burn. The flame burned for eight days. No one thought it would last for more than a few hours—maybe a day at the most. The Maccabees wondered at this flame lasting so long. There was only oil from one small jar. But a miracle occurred and the flame burned for eight days. It kept them company, as if God were working alongside them.

Finally, on the 25th day of the month of Kislev, 165 B.C.E., the Temple was finished. It had been prepared so God could visit again. It had been rededicated to God. That is what Chanukah means.

This made the Maccabees so happy that they celebrated the miracle of the oil and the rededication of the

Temple for eight days. Who would have thought that the flame would burn for so long? But then who would have thought that a small group of courageous Jews could win such a battle for freedom against the powerful armies of Antiochus?

The First Night

The Picture in the Flame

An Eastern European Tale

Tzil. Walotsky

he room was dark and silent. I waited. I felt my heart beating. Then there was the scratch of a match and a flash of light. I could see my grandmother, my Bubbe, as she held the match before her face. She lit the *shammash* candle and used it to kindle the one lonely candle that stood all alone in the *menorah* on this first night of Chanukah.

Bubbe whispered, "*Baruch atah Adonai eloheinu melech ha-olam asher kidshanu b-mitzvosav v'tzivanu l'hadlik neir shel Chanukah.*" She stood before the *menorah* and stared at the flame of the first candle. Her eyes began to fill with tears, but she did not blink. She looked so sad, so very far away in thought.

My grandfather, my Zaide, came up behind her and

15

hugged her close to him. He quietly finished the remaining two blessings recited on the first night of Chanukah. Bubbe clutched the two hands that hugged her.

Mother turned on the kitchen light. The shadows disappeared from the wall. Bubbe turned her face to Zaide and they hugged.

"Don't worry about your bubbe's tears," said Zaide as he noticed me standing beside them. "Each year on the first night of Chanukah, your Bubbe looks into the flame of that first candle and sees it filled with a very special memory."

I hurried back to the kitchen table, climbed onto a chair, and raised myself up on both knees so I would be as tall as that first candle. I wanted to know what Bubbe saw.

"What do you think, Sarah?" Zaide asked Bubbe. "It's time to tell him."

"Come here, bubeleh," invited Bubbe. She picked me up and carried me into the living room and placed me on her knees as she sat down.

"Look outside," Bubbe began as she pointed to the window. "It was a night just like tonight, many, many years ago."

"We lived in a small village called a *shtetl*. Our home was small, too. It had only two rooms. One was a bedroom for my mama and papa. The other was a kitchen and living room all in one.

"My brother Chayim, my sister Esther, and I slept on straw mattresses. We would huddle together in front of the big stove in the kitchen.

"It was the first night of Chanukah and we were busy getting ready. We had to wash the walls, and sweep the floor and cover it with a new layer of straw. Chayim had to bring in the wood from outside to keep the fire burning in the stove. Mama was cooking. She cooked all day. Most of the time we ate only bread, onions, some milk, and a few vegetables. But as if by magic, Mama always had some treats for the holidays. For Chanukah she made little cakes and wonderful *latkes*. All day long the whole house smelled of potatoes and onions frying.

"It was very cold. The wind howled and crept into the house through cracks in the walls and from under the door. If you stepped too far away from the stove, you felt a chill that made you shiver.

"We were dressed in our holiday clothes, waiting for Papa to come home. He was a woodcutter and had taken a cartload of wood to the home of a customer.

"We knew that he should have been home by now. He was always home in time to begin the holidays. Mama said nothing. She scurried back and forth between the kitchen stove and the kitchen table. Finally she sat down in her wooden chair and picked up her sewing. I loved to watch her as she slipped the needle in and out of the material, pausing every now and then to moisten the tip of a new thread in her mouth and pass it through the eye of the needle.

"When the wind rattled the front door, we would look up anxiously hoping that it was Papa. But it was only the wind. Papa was still out there in the snow somewhere trying to get home to us.

"Eventually, the time came to light the *menorah*, but none of us said a word to Mama. We would light it when Papa came home.

17

"Outside we heard the voices of some of the men singing on their way home from the *shtibl* after Evening Prayers. Even though the wind howled, the *niggunim* of the men could be heard clearly.

"If only your Papa could hear the *niggunim*," Mama whispered like a prayer.

"Suddenly, Mama grabbed her shawl and draped it over her head and around her shoulders. She ran outside. What was she doing? Why did she run outside into the bitter cold, snowy night? We waited.

"The front door crashed open and a gust of wind rushed inside. It rattled the rickety wooden table and pushed the old rocking chair back and forth.

"Mama told us to get our coats and follow her, quickly. We left the house, and immediately our eyes began to water from the cold. Our faces grew red, and we pulled up our scarves to cover our mouths and noses. We scurried behind Mama as she led us through the *shtetl*, past the butcher shop and the marketplace. The snow was up to our knees and we had to lift our legs high in the air as we trudged along.

"Finally we reached the *shtibl*. As we opened the door to enter, snow blew in and made the faded floor boards wet. The *shtibl* had only one room, like most of the houses. In the middle was a raised platform surrounded by wooden railings. To the left were bookshelves filled with old books. Straight ahead, mounted like a cabinet onto the eastern wall, was the Ark. It had a scarlet velvet curtain across its front, and inside, hidden by the curtain, was the sacred Torah. Low wooden benches were scattered throughout the room.

"More people came in after us, and soon the little

room was filled. The whole town was there. Reb Avreml the tailor, Reb Moyshe the baker, Reb Shlomo the *shochet*—everyone was there.

"In the midst of this throng was our *rebbe*. He wore his long black coat and sat behind one of the long narrow tables in the center of the room. He lifted his head and looked out at all of us through eyes as black as coal. He did not blink. His beard was white and reached all the way to his chest.

"I was worried. Why were we here and what was our rebbe about to do?

"Then, in a haunting, trembling voice, the *rebbe* began that mysterious singsong chant called a *niggun*.

"'*Ya bah-bah, ya-bah-bah. Yei-be-be-be-bah....*'

"And almost without realizing it, we began to sing with the *rebbe*. Our bodies swayed back and forth to the beat of the mysterious melody. The *shtibl* shook and vibrations ran along the floor boards.

"'*Ya bah-bah, ya-bah-bah....*'

"We held on to each other and sang louder and louder.

"'*Ya bah-bah, ya-bah-bah....*'

"My eyes glimpsed the *menorah* in the center of the room. The vibrations in the room made the flame dance on the surface of the oil.

"Then the singing stopped. All of a sudden there was silence. The *rebbe* had stopped, and as one voice we stopped, too. No one said a word.

"The *rebbe* opened his eyes and looked beyond us to the door. As his glance reached the door, it burst open.

"'Dovid!' cried Mama.

"'Papa!' we cried, and ran with Mama to hug him.

19

"He shivered as we held on to him. His dark beard was hidden by frost and ice. We held onto him and hugged."

"David," said Bubbe as she turned from the window and looked at me. "You were named for my father."

"Bubbe," I asked. "What happened?"

"It was a miracle. My father had been traveling home in that storm all day. It was snowing so hard he could not see even two feet in front of him. When it grew dark he almost gave up all hope of ever finding his way home. And then he heard music. He heard singing. Just like Mama thought, the sound of our voices singing in the *shtibl* reached him and guided him home.

"So you see, David, Chanukah was a time of miracles for the Maccabees and it was a time of miracles for your Bubbe, too. Whenever I light that first candle in the *menorah*, I see a picture of my papa in the flame. Maybe someday when you grow older, you'll look into that first flame and you'll see a picture of your Bubbe. The flames hold memories."

I jumped down from Bubbe's lap and ran to the kitchen table. For a long time I stared into the flame of that first candle. Would I see a picture someday, too?

HANUKKAH NIGUN

English Text: C.D.

Arr. by Charles Davidson

22

23

The Second Night

The Secret of the Shammash

A Sephardi Tale

In the ancient city of Constantinople lived a Jewish doctor by the name of Nissim Rahamim. He was a scholar and a beloved physician well known to all for his wise and kind treatment of his patients.

When news of this doctor reached the ears of the Sultan, he began to ask many questions about Nissim. The Sultan was always asking questions, because he was so curious about everything in the world, and was surrounded by many wise men who knew many things. One day, the Sultan summoned Nissim Rahamim to come before him, and as they spoke, the Sultan became amazed at Nissim's wisdom and ways. At the conclusion of their meeting the Sultan appointed Nissim to be his personal physician. As time went by, Nissim and the Sultan be-

came friends. Not only would Nissim visit the Sultan in the palace, but the Sultan would also visit Nissim at his home.

It so happened that on the last night of Chanukah, the Sultan came for a visit. When he entered the house, he saw the glow of the Chanukah lamp and was filled with a happiness he had not felt before. He saw the whole family sitting around the table eating pancakes and playing with a spinning top. The doctor welcomed the guest and invited the Sultan to sit at the table with them, offering to teach him to play the game of *dreidle*. Immediately, the Sultan drew his chair closer and accepted the offer.

"You see that each of us has a pile of nuts that we use in place of coins. Each one takes a turn spinning the *dreidle*, which has a Hebrew letter engraved on each side. Each letter, *nun, gimmel, hey, shin*, stands for a Hebrew word. When the *dreidle* falls on the *nun*, nothing happens, and no one wins or loses any nuts. When it falls on *gimmel*, then that player wins all the nuts in the middle. *Hey* means that the player receives half the nuts. *Shin* means that the player loses and puts all his nuts into the middle."

The Sultan listened carefully and soon was playing easily and often the *dreidle* would fall on *gimmel*. "You say that the Hebrew letters stand for words. What words, Nissim?"

"They stand for '*Nes Gadol Haya Sham*,' which means 'A Great Miracle Happened There,'" answered Nissim.

"A miracle? What miracle?" asked the Sultan.

So Nissim told the Sultan about the Maccabees and why they fought and how they defeated the armies of

30

Antiochus. Then he continued his narrative explaining how the Jews arrived at the Temple in Jerusalem and how they rededicated it with the holy oil.

"The miracle? It was all a miracle from God, but the miracle of renewed hope and rededication, of a little pot of oil that continued to burn for eight days instead of for the expected one day, the miracle that this reminded us that we Jews are a light to the world, all of these are the miracle of Chanukah," answered Nissim. "Since that time, we celebrate and remember to rededicate ourselves just as the Maccabees did in those times. Ah, but now it is your turn to spin the *dreidle*." And Nissim gave the Sultan the *dreidle* and the playing continued.

The Sultan looked carefully around the room in between his turns. He noticed the Chanukah lamp, which stood on a table near the door. "Why do you place the lamp near the door? Why not in the center of the main table, here?" asked the Sultan.

Nissim explained, "The *chanukiah*, as we call the Chanukah lamp, is placed near the door so that it is near the *mezuzah*. Since it is a *mitzvah* to light the candles each of the nights of the festival, by placing the lamp near the door post, there is a *mitzvah* on both sides of the door."

They continued playing the game of *dreidle*, but the Sultan, curious about the many new things around him, asked, "And why do you have so many candles?"

And Nissim told him that there were eight days of the festival because the little cruse of oil lasted for eight days. "So we burn an additional candle for each night of the holiday until all eight candles are burning bright, just as you see here on this last night of Chanukah."

But the Sultan raised his eyebrows and looked again at

the *chanukiah*, counting the candles. "But I see a ninth candle that is placed higher than the others. Why is that?"

"This candle is not counted as part of the eight. It is called the *shammash*. It is the servant that is used to light the other candles. But we place it higher than the others. We are not permitted to use the light of the candles. So when we enjoy their light, we can say we enjoy the light of the *shammash*," answered Nissim.

But the Sultan was still not satisfied with this explanation. "I am certain that there is a hidden meaning to the *shammash* or else why would you keep it lighted, and why on a higher level? Perhaps there is a secret that you do not wish to tell me? That is known only between Jews?"

But before Nissim could deny this, the Sultan continued, "Come to the palace in three days time and reveal the secret of the *shammash*." And with these words, the Sultan stood up, bid good night to the family, and left the house.

What was Nissim to do? What could he tell the Sultan about the "secret of the *shammash*," since there was no secret? He had read and studied all the works in the Talmud, and he had never heard of any secret. Should he make up something that might satisfy the Sultan? For the next two days, the doctor's thoughts were filled with this dilemma.

On the night of the second day Nissim decided to take a walk in the cool air. It was so quiet that he could hear the echo of his own footsteps. Suddenly an old man was walking beside him. Nissim had not heard him. He had not noticed him before. They walked for a while in silence. Then turning to Nissim, the old man said, "Well, Nissim, who will carry whom?"

Nissim looked at the old man curiously and wondered if he was crazy. I might be able to carry you, he thought, but you are much too old and frail to carry me. Nissim did not reply, thinking that perhaps he had not heard the man correctly.

After a while, they passed a house from which sounds of weeping could be heard. The coffin near the door told them this was a house of mourning. As they passed, the old man turned to Nissim and asked, "Do you think the man in the coffin is alive or dead?"

Now Nissim understood that the old man was confused and decided not to answer a madman.

As they continued on the walk, they passed a field where the wheat was ready for reaping. "What full ears of wheat! But I would like to know if it has already been eaten," said the old man.

Again Nissim did not know how to reply, and only shrugged his shoulders.

After a while, they turned and walked back in the direction of Nissim's house. As they came to a large house, the old man said, "This is a pleasant house, but I wonder if there are living creatures in this house."

Nissim could no longer restrain himself. He laughed and said, "This is my house. Come in and rest awhile. Refresh yourself with a cup of coffee and see for yourself if the people are living." Nissim hoped the old man would accept his invitation so that perhaps he would explain the strange remarks he had made during their walk.

The old man entered the house and gratefully accepted a cup of coffee. Drinking the strong coffee, Nissim was

33

also refreshed, as he had not rested for these past two days thinking of how to solve the riddle of the *shammash*.

He turned to his guest and asked, "What did you mean by your remark about living creatures when we reached my house?"

And the old man smiled, saying, "Living creatures means children. And when there are children who are full of joy and life, and the parents bring them up with the love of Torah, then the children keep their joy of life forever."

When Nissim heard this, his heart was filled with a happy feeling and he answered, "Baruch haShem, Blessed be God for He has given us beautiful children, but they are asleep now."

Now Nissim was more assured that the stranger was not out of his mind, but rather filled with a deep wisdom. And so he continued to question the old man.

"Your words puzzled me, my friend. What did you mean when we passed the wheat field and you wondered whether the crop had already been eaten?"

And the old man answered, "Some people spend more than they earn, so I wondered if the people who owned the wheat field had debts they would have to pay with the crop. Thus, the crop would belong to someone else even before it is reaped."

"I understand. And what did you mean by asking if the man in the coffin was alive or dead? That seems to be an obvious choice," asked Nissim cautiously.

"Not at all. You see, when a person lives like a man and not like an animal, when he studies Torah and keeps the commandments and does good deeds, then he lives forever. His good deeds and acts of loving-kindness live

34

after him. When his body dies, his soul survives and continues to live in eternal life. People remember him for good. In Safed, the righteous are buried in that part of the cemetery called *Beit HaHaim*, the House of the Living. And so the wicked are dead even in their lifetime, but the righteous, even after their death, are called 'living.'"

Now Nissim came to the one remaining question. "What did you mean when you asked who would carry whom? That didn't seem to make any sense at all."

The old man laughed a little and answered, "When people travel together, and the way seems long and hard, they tell stories or sing songs, or have a discussion on a point of Talmud. Then the way seems shorter and the traveling lighter, as though one traveler were carrying the other. So what I was asking was who will begin telling something interesting to the other?"

What appeared to be so mysterious to Nissim a few moments before now became so easy to understand. He also apologized to the old man for thinking that he was perhaps foolish or even mad.

Then they sat in silence. After a while, the old man leaned over and said to Nissim, "I see that something is troubling your soul. As Solomon said, 'A man should speak of the anxiety in his heart to help lighten it.'"

Sensing that this man had the power to understand, Nissim thought that perhaps he could help him with his problem. He then told the old man about the Sultan's visit and his command to appear before him to explain the secret of the *shammash*. "I tried to explain about the *shammash* to the Sultan, but he accused me of withholding something from him. What can I tell him tomorrow? What secret does the *shammash* contain?"

The old man sat for a moment, looking as though he had been expecting this question. "Tell the Sultan that this is the secret of the *shammash*. The *shammash* stands up high to look out and announce the following: 'Everyone look at me. I was once stored in a juicy fruit called the olive. When I grew and almost burst, I called out, "Pick me, put me into an olive press, take my oil to the last drop so I can live and be useful." So they came and plucked me from the tree, put me into the olive press, threw away my outer skin, and saved my inner part, my soul. And now I burn with a happy light that drives away darkness. Learn from me.' And so we must do what the *shammash* tells us. We must help to spread Torah and light. We must help the weak and oppressed. We must help the needy and teach those who do not know. In this way, you will also rise to a higher level and the world will benefit from you."

As Nissim listened, tears appeared in his eyes and he wept. After a while, he raised his head and turned to thank the old man. But he had vanished. "He must have been Elijah the Prophet," Nissim said with wonder and a grateful heart.

Now that he had learned the secret of the *shammash*, he could go to the Sultan with the answer to his question.

The Third Night

Chanukah Means Hope

A Holocaust Tale

Many years ago, our town was the nicest place to live. Trees lined the streets and wooden carts filled with fruit and vegetables stood by the curbs. On Thursday nights, we would go to the bakery and buy the *challahs* that had just emerged from the brick ovens. We always bought three *challahs*, two to eat on *Shabbos* and one to eat on the way home. Fresh from the oven, it was so sweet and warm it seemed to melt on our tongues.

I studied violin with Mr. Solomon. He was a kind man with chubby cheeks that would puff up and push his eyes closed whenever he smiled. Mr. Solomon thought that I might grow up to be a great violinist, if only I would practice more. But I did not like to practice.

One day, the Nazi soldiers came to our town.

41

"Don't worry," Mama said to us, "the Nazis won't stay here long. They are on their way to somewhere else, and they just decided to stop here for a while. They'll be gone soon." But Mama did not look directly at us when she spoke, so I knew she did not mean what she said.

One Thursday evening we were all on our way to the bakery, Mama and Papa and my little sister Necha.

"What's that?" cried Papa suddenly. And we all looked up to where he was pointing. The bakery window had been smashed and black smoke was coming from inside. "Quick," I called out, "we must see if Mr. Geller is all right."

I ran before Mama could grab me and when I got to the bakery, I stopped short. There was broken glass everywhere, the little pieces glistening in the moonlight like crystals. All the cakes had been thrown off the shelves. The *challahs* had been torn to pieces and strewn throughout the shop.

As I turned to leave, my way was blocked by a creature in black. I stared at the high black boots, at the black uniform, and at the shiny black helmet with the swastika gleaming at me. It was a Nazi soldier.

"What are you doing here?" he snapped. "Are you a friend of the Jewish baker?"

I was so frightened that I couldn't speak. I opened my mouth but my throat was so dry that nothing came out.

"Get out of here!" ordered the Nazi, and he kicked me with one of his boots.

With tears in my eyes, I ran to Mama and Papa. Together we fled back to our house.

The Monsters in Black Boots built a high wall around our town and locked us in with a huge iron gate. Then the trucks started coming, bringing Jews from smaller neighboring towns.

"Where can they live?" asked Mama. "We must take as many as we can to stay with us. Can we allow them to live in the street?"

Two families came to live in our tiny apartment. Six other children shared the bedroom that Necha and I had always had to ourselves. We took turns sleeping in the beds and on the floor.

On Sundays, we used to go to the school auditorium and watch a play. Sometimes my theater club was involved, and I had a chance to stand on the big stage in front of the whole town. Now there were people living on the stage. The town was so crowded that the school became a place for the homeless to live. So did the gymnasium and the movie house.

Chanukah was coming. We used to have big parties and invite our friends. Mama would bake *kugel* and fry *latkes*, and Papa would organize *dreidle* games. Every player was given twenty raisins to start the game. Everyone began by putting two raisins in the middle to form one large pile. Then each player got a turn to spin the wooden *dreidle*. Each letter on the *dreidle* had a meaning. If the *dreidle* landed on the letter *nun*, which means *nisht*, then the spinner got nothing. *Gimmel* stands for *gantz*, which meant that the spinner got all the raisins in the pile. *Hey* meant that the spinner could take *halb*, or half, of the pile of raisins, and *shin* meant that the spinner had to put, *shtel*, all the raisins from his own pile into the pile in the middle. Oh, how we loved that *dreidle* game.

But this year there would be no party. There would be

43

no *dreidle* game. There would be no celebrations of any kind.

I sat at my bedroom window and looked into the night sky. It was very dark. There was no moon and no stars. The street was bleak and deserted. The Nazis had ordered the streetlights to be extinguished early.

Papa opened the door. Quietly, he climbed over the other sleeping children and sat down next to me on the bed.

"What are you looking at?" he whispered.

He put his arm around me, and I started to cry.

"Sometimes things can look very dark and very frightening," he said softly. "But watch this."

And he took a match out of his pocket.

"Do you see how dark it is in this room?" he asked. I nodded.

"Well then, watch how one small match can chase away all the darkness."

Papa struck the match against the wooden window sill. Suddenly, a flame arose and danced on the match head. It cast its light across the whole room. I saw the other children asleep on the floor, their mouths slightly open as they snored softly, deep in their world of dreams.

"Tomorrow is Chanukah," said Papa. "We Jews have always believed in the power of light. Remember that our prophet Isaiah said that we were a light to the other nations of the world. Even one Jew who believes can chase the darkness of evil from the world. Antiochus was like these Nazis. He thought he could make us give up being Jews. He thought it would be easy to destroy us. But Judah Maccabee and his brothers believed in the strength of our people. Judah and the other Maccabees

44

were only one small candle against the darkness of Anti-ochus's whole army. But they chased the wicked Anti-ochus away, just like this match I am holding chases the darkness from this room. Every time a Jew lights a candle, as we do on Chanukah, we chase away some of the evil in the world."

Papa hugged me and left the room. But he left something behind. I could feel a thin stick next to me on the bed. When I picked it up, I saw it was a match. It felt like a magic wand in my hand. As long as I had it, I could banish darkness and defeat the demons of the world.

The next day the deportations began. We were herded onto trucks like cattle. The Monsters in Black Boots used sticks and attack dogs to squeeze us into the trucks.

The trucks carried us to the train. So many of us were packed into the train cars that we had to stand. None of us had eaten all day.

Necha cried most of the way. "Mama, Mama. I can't breathe. It's so hot in here. Papa, do something."

What could Papa do? What could any of us do?

Rabbi Hirsch had become very sick. Even though we were packed very tightly in the train, we made room for him to lie down with his head resting against the wall.

I looked up at Papa's worried face. He and Mama whispered to each other and touched each other's cheeks tenderly. Mama's eyes were filled with tears. When they thought Necha or I was looking at them, they smiled and told us that we would be all right.

"What's to worry?" said Mama. "We are all together, right? At least we're all together."

We stood in the moving train for hours. None of us knew where we were going.

45

Some of the children began to cry from hunger. Mama and several other parents dug deep into their pockets, where they had smuggled some bread, a potato or two, and some butter.

"It's important for you to keep your strength up," she said as she handed me a slice of potato.

I took the potato and squeezed my way over to the rabbi. Maybe if he had something to eat he would feel better. But his eyes were dull, nearly lifeless, and he waved his hand feebly, as if to say that he had no desire to eat, or even to live anymore, for that matter.

It was evening. I could see the darkness through a crack in the wooden wall of the train.

"Rabbi," I said. "It is *erev Chanukah*. Shouldn't we say the blessings and sing *Maoz Tzur*?"

"Where is the *menorah* to kindle?" asked the rabbi. "And what miracle shall we ask God for?"

Chanukah is the festival of lights. Without lights there was no miracle to proclaim. We had barely enough time to get our coats when the Monsters in Black Boots chased us from our homes, much less collect our *menorahs*. Then I remembered the slice of potato in my hand.

First I hollowed out a tiny well in its middle, and when that was done, I pulled the lace out of my right shoe.

"Mama, please let me have some butter. Please, Mama, let me have a small piece of butter."

Seeing the desperation in my eyes, Mama reached into her pocket for the small stick of butter she had taken when we were deported. I broke off a piece and made my way back to where the rabbi lay against the wall.

In my pocket was the match that Papa had given me the night before. With one short scrape against the

46

wood, a flame arose and danced on the match head. As I held the flame to the butter it began to melt, and the fat dripped into the well I had made in the potato. I placed my shoelace in the potato like a candle wick and used the dying match flame to light the lace.

"Rabbi," I cried. "Here is your *menorah*."

Rabbi Hirsch opened his eyes wide in wonder. The flame reflected in his eyes as if two smaller flames had just been kindled in his soul. Slowly he began to sit up, never blinking and never taking his eyes off the flame.

"*Baruch ata Adonai*," he whispered. And all the crying in our train stopped. "*Eloheinu melech ha-olam, asher kidshanu b-mitzvosav v-tzivanu l-hadlik neir shel chanukah*."

"Amen," I said. "Amen," echoed the rabbi. He was sitting up, eyes sparkling. As he recited the other blessings, he rose to his feet. It was a miracle of Chanukah.

We sang *Maoz Tzur* and *Mi Yemaleil* with such power and energy that the train started to rock back and forth. There we were, prisoners herded onto the train of the Monster. Yet, that night, the spirit of Chanukah rocked the train.

I looked at Papa. "One candle can defeat all the darkness," I said.

Papa smiled at me and pulled me close to him.

My one candle had banished all the darkness in our lives that night. And for many dark nights to come, I kept the memory of that candle burning inside me.

The Fourth Night

A Secret Chanukah

A Marrano Tale

nce, in the dark days of King Ferdinand and Queen Isabella of Spain, there lived a young girl named Francisca. Fate was not kind to her, for of all times in which to be born, she was born in Spain during the misery of the Inquisition. It was an age of great evil and persecution. For years Jews who observed their holidays, or sought God in prayer, or endeavored to teach their children the heritage of their ancestors were imprisoned and often executed upon a burning stake.

In August of 1492, Francisca had stood upon the dock and watched as the great Christopher Columbus set sail for the New World. She had longed to go with him and escape her life of suffering. She prayed for someone to rescue her and all the other secret Jews. Perhaps, she

53

thought, in the New World things were different. Could it be that the New World was really God's Garden of Eden, a paradise where there were no Inquisitors and where people loved one another? Francisca had remained on the dock long after the Nina, the Pinta, and the Santa Maria had left the harbor. She watched each of the ships sail out to sea and slowly disappear into the horizon. Even when she could no longer see the huge white sails filled with the ocean breeze, she continued to gaze out over the blue waters.

Now it was winter. *Kislev* had come to the world. Francisca and her family knew it was time for Chanukah, but they also knew that if they were caught lighting the *chanukiah* they could be imprisoned, or worse.

One night, toward the very end of the month of *Kislev*, Francisca lay asleep in her bed. A brilliant moon visited the world that night and three stars appeared in the sky above the town. A breeze stirred, and softly tapped at the shutters to Francisca's window. Gently, it loosened the latch and the shutters swung open. The breeze floated through the room and stroked Francisca's face with its cool touch. It beckoned to Francisca to ride its invisible wave to lands far away.

Francisca was not sure she wished to embark on such a nocturnal journey, but the breeze was persistent, and finally, she agreed. Up, up she rose and floated out the window.

For just a moment, she hovered over the town, marveling at the stillness in the streets. All the houses were dark. No one moved. Cats called to one another. Night birds sang their quiet songs.

Then, in an instant, Francisca found herself soaring through the skies. She flew over towns, over tall mountains, and through wide valleys. As she passed one of the mountaintops, she reached down to scoop up some snow from the peak.

On and on she traveled on the back of the wind. How free she felt! She soared like a bird. For half the night, she flew. Then finally the wind began to calm down and Francisca floated softly down to earth. She landed just outside the mouth of a deep, dark cave.

Gently, the breeze pushed Francisca inside the cave. For several moments, she could not see at all. It was as black as the blackest of nights, but somehow she did not bump into anything even once. After a while, she came to a room deep inside the cave. In the middle of the room there was a fire burning, and around the fire, sitting on thrones, were five figures dressed in robes, their faces hidden from view by their hoods.

"Francisca, the breeze has brought you to us," said one of the figures.

"We have heard your prayers," said another.

"We have a gift for you," said a third.

Then they each removed their hoods. The glow of the fire filled their eyes and, even though it was very dark in the cave, it was easy to see each of the five men.

Francisca was astonished.

"I am Judah Maccabee," said the first man. "Next to me sit my four brothers. God has given us the task of tending this fire. It is a special flame kindled by a spark from the Divine throne. It is the light of God. Those who are comforted by its warmth find courage and hope."

55

Francisca gazed at the crackling flame. She could feel its warmth.

"When we first began our struggle against the tyrant Antiochus," said Judah, "we hid from his soldiers in caves. One night, after a battle, we sat in a cave nursing all our comrades who had been wounded in the day's fighting. It was cold in the cave and dark. No matter how we tried, we could not keep the wind from putting out our fire. That night, for the first and only time, I wondered if we could actually prevail. Could we defeat the most powerful army in the world? Then I remembered the words from the Torah: '*Mi Chamocha Baelim Adonai?* Who is like our God among all of the false gods of the other nations?' Those words gave me courage. They gave me strength. I knew at that moment that if we believed in the power of Adonai, our God, we would win. Suddenly, our sputtering flame rose and roared. No matter how hard the wind blew that night, the flame continued to burn. The fire was so bright and warm, it made us all feel brave. After that night, we never were fearful again. The next day, we defeated Antiochus's army and recaptured the Temple."

Judah stopped speaking and walked toward Francisca. He placed his hands on her shoulders and looked deeply into her eyes.

"We know that you and your family cannot kindle the lights of the *chanukiah* this year. Do not be sad, and do not despair. Turn to the flames, Francisca, and study them well."

Francisca watched the flames rise and fall. She studied every part of their dance. She memorized the reds, oranges, yellows, whites, and blues that appeared in the

56

fire. She followed every spark that flew out and disappeared into the dark night.

"Now close your eyes," whispered Judah. "Can you still see the flame in your mind."

Francisca nodded her head. She did not dare speak for fear that her voice would shatter the magic of this moment.

"God's light will always be with you. When you are frightened or sick at heart, all you need to do is close your eyes and find God's light. Tonight is the fourth night of Chanukah. When you are alone in your room and three stars have appeared in the sky, close your eyes and find the lights of God's fire. Feel its warmth. Feel your courage. Then imagine that you have your family's *chanukiah* before you. Take hold of the *shammash* and thrust it into God's fire. Use this flame to light the four candles in your *chanukiah*. This is your secret. No one can ever take this flame from you. It will always be there for you whenever you need hope or courage."

A gust of wind blew through the shutters and lifted the covers from Francisca's sleeping body and awakened her. She shivered. She was no longer in the cave with the Maccabees. Here she was back in her bed. Had she been dreaming?

The moon was shining and spreading its soft white glow over the surface of the street outside. Stars twinkled and sparkled. Then she remembered about the flame. She closed her eyes and the flame appeared just as Judah said it would. She imagined her family's *chanukiah* with the *shammash* in its place and four other candles standing tall, awaiting their kindling flame.

Francisca used the flame to kindle her *chanukiah*. Then she opened her eyes and looked at the stars once more. What if her evening's adventure had really been a dream?

No matter, she thought. God's light is very real. This Chanukah, she knew she had been given a secret gift. One that she would keep forever.

The Fifth Night

How To Sell
a Menorah!

An Eastern European Tale

Hershele Ostropolier the prankster was always looking for new ways to make a few kopeks. Not that he had any intention of working for a living—Heaven forbid! Rather, he earned by his wits and his tongue. After all, he had been appointed jester to Rabbi Boruch of Miedziboz and he had to keep finding new ways and words to lift the rabbi out of his melancholia. But he also had to invent ways to match wits with the rabbi in order to get his wages. More often than not, as a matter of fact, he did not get paid. Then Hershele would say to himself, "My name isn't Hershele for nothing. Take advantage of me, and you'll pay dearly for it." What would Hershele do? Doing what he did best, he would tell the rabbi a good story, a story with such convoluted logic,

yet with such a clear lesson, that in the end, the rabbi became shamed into paying Hershele his wages.

Always a pauper, always fighting poverty, Hershele was also always hungry. Once he went into an inn for a meal. Seeing this desheveled, scary looking fellow, the innkeeper's wife, who was alone in the inn, became frightened and refused to serve him. "We have no more food left in the kitchen," she said.

"Well, then, I'll have to do what my father always did," announced Hershele in a loud voice.

Becoming even more alarmed by what he might do, the innkeeper's wife ran to the kitchen and brought out a veritable feast. Hershele ate with a hearty appetite. Then, as she watched Hershele drinking his glass of tea, the innkeeper's wife, feeling more calm, approached him and asked in a timid voice, "So what would your father always do?"

With a big grin, Hershele replied, "When my father had no food, he went hungry."

Now Hershele was hardly a lazy man, for it was more than a full-time job for him to avenge all the insults he received, wheedle money (even from his wife!), outsmart unsuspecting innkeepers for a meal, and especially when he was slighted or rebuffed, even teach a greedy man or rogue a lesson.

"Just you wait, you rogue! My name isn't Hershele for nothing! Insult me to your heart's content, you'll pay dearly for it."

Hershele never used violence to achieve his goals. His weapon was words, and the arrow always reached its mark. Not only did the person learn the lesson, but Hershele gained a meal, or a few kopeks, at the same time. The saying "He who laughs last, laughs best" could have been invented just for Hershele.

Hershele was thinking very hard about his next few kopeks, particularly where they would come from. "Holidays are especially good times for earning a few kopeks," he thought. "And there are certainly plenty of holidays. Soon it will be Chanukah. Chanukah. . . . Of course! What does every Jew need for Chanukah? *A menorah!*"

So Hershele set out to find a tinmaker who would make a bagful of *menorahs* for him, all of the same size and design. Finally he found one who—unbelievably—agreed to his terms. The tinmaker would give Hershele the *menorahs* on consignment; after Hershele got paid, the tinmaker would get paid.

During the last few days before Chanukah, Hershele went around town selling his *menorahs*. On the morning before Chanukah, with only a few *menorahs* left, Hershele entered the shop of a wealthy shopkeeper who was as stingy as he was rude. Hershele pulled a *menorah* from his bag and placed it on the table. "It's time to buy the *menorah*," he said. "And this is the finest one I have, especially suited for such a prominent citizen as yourself. I have saved this one just for you."

The wealthy shopkeeper barely glanced up from his books and replied, "No, no, I'm not interested. I have a *menorah* from last year that will do just fine. My wife will find it and prepare it for lighting."

But Hershele was not to be put off by a simple no. "Do you like *latkes*?" he asked.

"I love *latkes*," replied the shopkeeper, patting his large stomach.

"Well then, can you imagine your wife searching all afternoon for the *menorah* and discovering, when she finally finds it, that one of the candle holders has broken off? Then what would she do? I'll tell you what she would do. She would have to search through the town for another *menorah*, and who knows if she could find one just before the holiday? By then, it would be almost dark. And then she wouldn't have time to peel all the potatoes and grate them and make the beautiful potato *latkes* you love so much. And what kind of *yom tov* would it be without lighting the candles and with no *latkes*? Think how sorry you would be that you didn't buy this *menorah* from me."

By now, all the shopkeeper wanted was to be rid of Hershele, so he bought the *menorah*.

Hershele quickly left the shop and rushed to the shopkeeper's house. When the shopkeeper's wife came to the door, Hershele was standing there with a *menorah* in his hand. "I just came from your husband's shop and he asked me to tell you not to look for last year's *menorah*. He said you should just buy a new one from me." Hershele held the *menorah* out to the shopkeeper's wife and, well, what could she do? She bought the *menorah* from Hershele.

That evening, the wealthy man arrived home with the *menorah* he had bought from Hershele safely bundled in layers of paper. When he had unwrapped it, he carried it into the living room for his wife to see. And there she stood, holding a *menorah* exactly like the one he carried.

"Where did you get that *menorah*?" questioned the husband.

"From Hershele, of course. Just as you told me to," answered the wife.

66

"I told you? Who told you?" the husband shouted. "Hershele! Hershele has tricked us both into buying from him!"

The wealthy man motioned angrily to his servant and said, "Find Hershele and bring him to me."

The servant went to Hershele's house, and finding him there, he said, "My master wants to see you immediately. Come quickly, before it's time to light the Chanukah *menorah*."

"Oh, your master must want to buy a *menorah* from me," said Hershele. "My *menorahs* are the best there are. But why did he wait until the last minute to buy one? By the time I go to his house and sell him a *menorah* and return home, it will be past the time to light the candles. So I'll tell you what. Why don't you just give me the money and I'll give you the *menorah* and *you* can take it to your master."

That's what happened. And that's how to sell a *menorah*!

Chanukah wicks total 9
The candles to light are 8
The days of the week are 7
The latkes to eat are 6
The pennies to give are 5
The sides of a dreidle are 4
Menorahs the miser bought are 3
The blessings over the candles are 2
And Hershele, master trickster is 1
And now the tale is done!

The Sixth Night

A Stranger's Gift

A Persian Tale

The sun was setting slowly in the west. Azaria stood outside his home looking up at the sky. It was streaked with colors as if God had taken a paintbrush and laced the heavens with purple, blue, red, and orange.

"Once the sun is all gone," said Azaria to himself, "another night of Chanukah will arrive."

Though Azaria was seven years old, he still had trouble adding and subtracting in his head. In order for him to figure out which night of Chanukah was coming, he had to count on his fingers.

"If the first night of Chanukah was also my brother Benjamin's birthday, how many nights would that be?" Azaria held out his hands and began counting on his fingers as he recalled each day since Benjamin's birthday.

73

"One, two, three, four, five, six. Six, that's it. Tonight is the sixth night of Chanukah!"

"Azaria, Azaria! What are you dreaming about?"

It was his mother calling. "It's time to light the *chanukiah*. Your father is waiting. Go to the cellar and get the olive oil."

It was a special olive oil used only for Chanukah. Azaria carefully brought the earthen pitcher upstairs and poured the clear, cool olive oil into the cups of the *chanukiah*. Seven cups. One for each of the six days and one for the *shammash*.

Azaria watched his father strike a long wooden match against the side of the table. As his father held the match aloft in front of him, its flame was reflected in his black eyes. He recited the blessings in a deep voice that sent tickling shivers up Azaria's spine.

Then, one by one, everyone kindled a wick in one of the cups, until finally Azaria's turn came. Since he was the youngest of four children, he had to wait until the sixth night to get a chance to light the *chanukiah*. That's why the sixth night would always be special for him.

After the *chanukiah* had been kindled and the blessings chanted, Azaria joined his family around the kitchen table. It was time for his father to tell the story of Chanukah.

Azaria loved the way his father told the story. He was also glad he was the youngest in the family. That meant that he got to sit on his father's lap as he told the story of the Maccabees.

Azaria thought it would have been wonderful to live in the time of the Maccabees. He knew he would have been

74

one of Judah Maccabee's soldiers. The wicked Antiochus did not scare him. How strong and brave Judah must have been! Azaria imagined himself standing with Judah right there in the midst of the battle to regain Jerusalem.

"Azaria! I need a brave soldier to lead my troops against Antiochus's armies," shouted Judah. "Will you do it? Only you can lead us to victory so we can recapture the holy Temple and make it ours again."

"Yes, General Judah. I will do it!" shouted Azaria. He hoisted his huge sword over his head and led the Maccabees against the Syrian armies. On, into the holy Temple he went. Nothing could stop him from rededicating the Temple to God. He would fix everything the Syrians had ruined: the torn curtains on the holy Ark, the candlesticks that had been turned over, and the sacred Torah scrolls which had been thrown on the ground. He would be a hero, just like Judah Maccabee.

Suddenly, he felt someone shaking him. It was his father.

"Azaria, you have been dreaming again. I have finished telling the story of Judah Maccabee. Now it's time for you to go and get your presents."

Azaria could not believe it. The dream seemed so real. He stretched on his father's lap and yawned. Slowly, he lowered himself to the ground and stood up. It was time to get his presents.

In Persia, where Azaria lived, children went from house to house collecting little gifts from their Jewish neighbors. Usually they were given bundles of roasted nuts and seeds. These were considered to be real treats.

As Azaria stepped outside his house, he heard his friends laughing as they compared the gifts in their bags. His brothers and sister had left a few minutes before him, and had already begun knocking on doors farther up the street. Azaria started to run to catch up to them, but after three steps he saw something that made him stop suddenly.

There in the road sat a single, lonely figure draped in a tattered robe. Azaria edged forward. He was afraid, but something about the mysterious stranger seemed familiar.

Azaria moved closer and noticed that under his bushy white beard, the stranger's skin was red and chapped. His eyes were sad and full of tears.

That's the man who sat in the back of the synagogue on *Shabbat*, thought Azaria. Even though he was dressed in rags, the rabbi treated him like an honored guest and gave him the special seat near the holy Ark.

Azaria's heart filled with sympathy for the nameless figure who stood shivering before him. He reached out and clasped the stranger's cold hand. In that moment when they held hands, Azaria knew what he had to do.

With great speed, he ran to the next house on his street. All the other children had already been there, but these neighbors had a bag of roasted seeds and nuts wrapped and waiting for him. Azaria thanked them, and ran back to the stranger and handed him the little bundle of Chanukah treats.

Then Azaria ran to the next house, and the next. Each time he thanked his neighbors for their kindness and turned his gift over to the stranger. It seemed like the only thing to do. The stranger needed these Chanukah gifts much more than he did. Besides, it made him feel better to give the stranger these presents than to keep them all to himself.

When Azaria reached the last house on his street, he turned to deliver his Chanukah gift to the stranger. But he was gone. Azaria searched up and down the road, but the stranger was nowhere to be found. He had disappeared as mysteriously as he had appeared. Azaria was confused. Was this just another one of his dreams? Perhaps there had really never been a stranger at all.

Azaria stood all alone in the middle of the street, his one small bag of nuts and seeds clutched tightly in his hand. When he returned home, his mother and father were waiting for him with a surprise.

"Azaria, while you were gone, someone came by and left this huge bag for you."

"Who was it?" asked Azaria.

"We do not know," replied his mother. "A great gust of wind blew through the house, rattling the glasses and causing the candles to flicker. Then there came a knock at the door. When we collected our wits and made our way to the door, there was no one to be seen. There was no one there at all. But we found this bag with your name written on it. We were just about to open it, when you came home."

Wide-eyed and with great enthusiasm, Azaria ripped open the bag. Its contents spilled to the ground, and the whole family gasped.

"I have never seen anything like it," cried Azaria's mother. "Nuts and seeds and candles—enough for a year!" But there was something else hidden amongst the treats.

77

"Gold coins!" cried Azaria. "Gold coins! One for each of us." Azaria knew that he had not been dreaming. But who could have brought such a gift? For many years he wondered about that gift and about the stranger he had helped on the street.

Then one day while he was studying, Azaria came upon a teaching that helped him understand this mystery: one who has helped a stranger may have helped an angel.

The Seventh Night

The Rescued Menorah

An American Tale

Let me tell you about what happened last summer as I was driving crosstown on East 37th Street in New York City. I was coming from the airport where I had picked up my cousin from London. He was going to visit us for a few weeks. Exiting from the Midtown Tunnel and heading west, I was in the middle of the block, between Third Avenue and Lexington Avenue, when the light at the corner turned red. I stopped the car and waited. On my right was a garbage truck. The garbage man had just emptied a garbage can into the back of the truck. As I was conversing with my cousin, I noticed from the corner of my eye that the man then reached into the truck and pulled out a shiny metal object. I looked directly at what he was holding in his hands and saw that

it was a brass Chanukah *menorah*. My mind raced. Signaling to my cousin to roll down the window, I called out, "Sir, that object you are holding in your hand is a religious object that belongs in a Jewish place." The garbage man came closer to the car and said, "Someone has just thrown this out—probably belonged to some old person."

Again I said, trying not to sound too eager, though speaking hurriedly, "But it is a religious object that should be in a synagogue, perhaps. Would you give it to me so I can bring it to a synagogue or give it to someone who would use it at holiday time?"

He examined the *menorah*, as though weighing it in both his hands and mind, perhaps realizing that it might have some value—or that it might serve as a nice candle holder for his home.

The light changed. Horns were beginning to sound, so I felt I had to move on. What else could I say? Would there be enough time to explain the *mitzvah* of returning this *menorah* to its proper use? How much money could I offer so he would sell it to me? Should I pull in front of his truck and plead my case more strongly? In the quickness of the moment, I just couldn't think fast enough.

Suddenly in my mind's eye, with a rush of memory, I was standing in my Bubbe and Zaide's apartment and together we were celebrating Chanukah.

My Bubbe and Zaide came from the old country. When I was a child I heard how they had come here to America, to a new country, a young country, and I decided they must have "thrown out" the old country, as if they had used it up or worn it out, like a neighbor who

84

had thrown away the welcome mat because another neighbor had worn it out. We had a mat in front of our door with the word WELCOME on it, and it never seemed to wear out. But maybe ours cost more. It was all very puzzling for a little girl. Maybe my grandparents and the rest of their big family had to leave Russia because there was no more room for anyone else. Why else would people leave their home, the place where they grew up, where their friends were? It certainly was confusing to me. But at that time I didn't know the right questions to ask to better understand the immigration of the Jews and the reasons why they had left their old home. However, as I grew older I became better at asking questions. I asked, "What's an old country?" and "Which old country?" and "What did they do with the old country?" and "Could they make it new again?" I heard them talking about how a country has a soul, so I said they could make it new by repairing the "soles," like on a pair of shoes.

"What do children know about such things?" said my parents. "When you grow up, you'll understand more. You'll have *seichel* and then you'll ask," they would add patiently smiling.

Wisdom must come automatically when you grow up, I reasoned. "But what age is grown-up?" I persisted.

They never could answer that question to my satisfaction. All they would tell me is, "You are grown-up when you have *seichel*!"

My Bubbe had a few things she had brought with her from her old home. She had several silver candlesticks, some gigantic feather quilts and pillows stuffed with goose feathers that she and her mother had themselves

plucked, and a *menorah* for Chanukah. The *menorah* was made of brass. It looked like a tree composed of four pairs of open arms. I loved that *menorah*. Every Chanukah, Bubbe would take it from the big glass cabinet, along with a smaller *menorah* for me, and place them on the table in front of the big window of her dining room, a room that faced the elevated railroad tracks on Park Avenue at the corner of 104th Street in New York City. Their third floor apartment, called a railroad apartment, probably because it was long like a railroad car, was in a brownstone at 1401 Park Avenue. This was a section of the city called Harlem, and in the 1930s and 1940s, many Jews lived there. Whenever a train rumbled by, everyone felt the vibrations and heard the noise. While the Chanukah candles were lit, the flames would dance even faster than usual, just for those few seconds. And when that happened, I would imagine to myself that it was Elijah walking by with his big cape flapping in the wind, causing the vibrations and checking to see if I had lit the candles and if I was watching them until they melted down and went out. Bubbe had always told me that it is a *mitzvah* to watch the candles once they are lit. "Remember," she would say in her Russian-Yiddish accent, "it is important to remember that watching the candles is part of the celebration of Chanukah with all its miracles. The little flames add joy and light. They give us a message from thousands of years ago. They are saying that once there is light, you will never accept darkness again. So, my Malkele, do not leave the room while the candles are burning because otherwise, if you leave the room and leave the candles alone, you will shame them." That's how Bubbe spoke. Always with a lesson, always with a proverb, always with the faith and beliefs of the Jewish people. Bubbe could never have been a child like me, she was always a wise old woman, with plenty of *seichel*. I was sure of that.

What I also liked about being in Bubbe's house during Chanukah were the *latkes* she made. "They are so delicious, Bubbe—even better than my mother's!" I would shout with a laugh, reaching for my tenth, or was it my twelfth *latke*?

"Sha, sha, my Malkele," my Bubbe would answer. "Your mama makes her *latkes* just like I do. She learned from me. But your mama is more modern than I am and knows how to cook better than me." But I would only smile and shake my head and hug my Bubbe tighter.

I also loved the stories Bubbe told. Whenever she was about to tell me a story, she would take off her flowered apron (my Bubbe loved roses so the apron had big roses all over it), sit in her favorite big cushioned chair near the *menorah*, and motion me to come sit next to her.

One Chanukah, when I was very young, Bubbe said, "I will tell you a story by Yehuda Leib Peretz, one of the great Yiddish writers." She explained that she had heard the story in the old country. I heard the story when I was young and this is how I remember it.

"Well, you see," she would start, "there was once a couple who lived happily together. They were poor, but happy. And when it came time for Chanukah, they would take their brass Chanukah lamp from its glass case and light the candles while they recited the blessings. That's how it was for years."

"What did the *menorah* look like, Bubbe?"

"Well, it had one twisted leg. There were brass birds in trees, and a big lion with its mouth open. Maybe it was laughing. On Chanukah even a lion is happy," she would say with a laugh that made the wrinkles on her face even deeper. Then she would continue, "And Shloime-Zalmen, that was the husband's name, one day found some kind of iron in the street. When he arrived home, he cleaned the iron and underneath he saw that it was made of gold. So now he was a rich man. Well, they changed their name, they changed the way they dressed, they changed their address, and the children also changed schools to go to a fancy private school—no more *yeshivas*. They sold everything they owned and bought fancy French high-toned antiques. They even gave away their holy books. But the circle keeps turning, and after a few years, they were no longer so rich. Things went from bad to worse—no use going into detail—but they could no longer afford the things they had been used to. Meanwhile, their sons were in schools in another country, in England, far away.

"Now when this couple was poor again, they remembered that they were Jews. So Shloime-Zalmen went to *shul* again. And when it was time for Chanukah, they remembered their old brass *menorah*. They searched everywhere for it hoping that maybe they hadn't thrown it away. In a corner near the stove, or maybe it was on top of the stove, they found it. Oh, they were so happy to see it, like a good old friend! They cleaned it and recited the blessings and lit the candles. They felt lighter in their hearts.

"One evening the doorbell rang and when they went to the door, standing there was an old furniture dealer they knew. 'Excuse me for disturbing you so late at night, but there is an Englishman who is an antique dealer and he is looking for old things to buy. Since I once bought old furniture from you, perhaps you still have some old things?' Standing behind the dealer was a man who looked like a *graf*, a nobleman. So Shloime-Zalmen invited them both in. As soon as the Englishman saw the Chanukah *menorah*, he said he wanted to buy it. 'How much do you want for that brass object?' he asked. And Shloime-Zalmen didn't know what to answer.

"He looked at his wife. She gave him the answer, but only with her eyes and a slight shake of her head from side to side. But he knew what she meant. 'No, no, thank you. We cannot accept your offer because it is Chanukah and we must light the candles each night. This is a *menorah* that we have had a long time. There must be a reason why we kept it, even when we didn't use it for a few years.'

"Soon after that night, things began to turn good again for this couple."

Many years have now gone by and my Bubbe and Zaide have died. I don't know what happened to my Bubbe's Chanukah *menorah*—Bubbe's *menorah*! Suddenly I knew that the *menorah* rescued from the garbage truck had reminded me of my Bubbe's *menorah*.

The car horns were deafening. Going with my impulse, I pulled in front of the garbage truck, got out of my car— reaching into my pocketbook at the same time, took out a large bill, and handed it to the man holding the *menorah*, hoping he would sell it to me.

"No, no, lady. I couldn't take any money for it. I'm a religious man myself. This is a Jewish candlestick, is it?

Then you take it and give it to someone who needs it and will use it. Good luck, and God bless you, lady.'' With a wave of his hand, he handed me the *menorah* and jumped onto the back of the garbage truck, smiling a great big smile.

Every year, that *menorah*—the *menorah* rescued on 37th Street—brings to my mind the *menorahs* of my childhood, the one at Bubbe's house and the one in her story. Did that discarded *menorah* really belong to an old person? Then who would have thrown it away? Maybe that person died and someone had come to clean out the apartment.

Oh, perhaps you want to know what happened to that *menorah*. I brought it to my rabbi and he gave it to a young couple who had just arrived from Soviet Russia to make a new life for themselves in America.

The Eighth Night
A Melody in Israel
An Israeli Tale

So what silly tune did you compose now, Dovidl? Let me hear it and I'll tell you if you should sing it at the Chanukah party in front of all those people."

"It's not a silly tune at all, Leahle," answered Dovid. "And I won't sing it for you now. No wonder your parents call you a *brenfire*. That's what you are."

"You know I'm only teasing you. Come on, do sing it. Or just play it on the piano and hum it. I won't say a word until you are through. I promise."

"All right," agreed Dovid eagerly. "Listen. It's a duet. I wrote it in honor of Chanukah. I used the words of *Haneiros Halalu*. We kindle these lights because of the wondrous deliverance You performed for our ancestors. I'll sing the first line, then like an echo, you'll sing the

95

second line. Then we join our voices in harmony on *al ha nissim*." Then with great delight, Dovid sat at the piano and began to play and sing his new composition.

Leah came closer and began to read the notes and sing with Dovid, and soon their voices grew stronger and surer—blending, harmonizing, joining together rhythmically. When they had finished, Dovid stood up and gave Leah a hug—and just as suddenly jumped back. "Forgive me, Leahle, I didn't mean to hug you. I mean, I should not have done that. I was just so happy to hear my song come to life, like when we first light the Chanukah candles. It's so beautiful, isn't it? Do you think so too, Leahle?"

Leah stood there, wanting to laugh, wanting to tease Dovid about the song, about the hug, even about his apology, but somehow, no sound came from her moving lips. Only the words, "Oh my beloved. The voice of my beloved!" came into her mind. She kept looking into Dovid's eyes, seeing him in a new way. The words of Song of Songs kept repeating in her mind, "*Behold, you are fair, my love, Behold, you are fair with your eyes as doves. And, oh, you are handsome, my lover, oh, sweet.*"

And Dovid, too, kept looking at Leah. He understood what Solomon meant when he wrote, "*How fair is your love, my sister, my bride.*" But he was also confused.

Leah had been like a sister all his life. They had known each other from the time they had been little children. Their houses were on the same street in their Eastern European town. They went to the same *heder*. Dovid loved music and they often sang together. Dovid was in the choir at the *shul*, and although girls were not permitted to sing

96

with the cantor and his choir, Leah learned all the melodies from listening and practicing with Dovid at home.

As Dovid grew older, he began writing down the melodies that were in his head with the help of his piano teacher and the cantor. Now Dovid could write his own music, even with piano chords. Dovid always shared his ideas and his music, and sometimes even his feelings, with his friend Leah. They had never thought about love . . . that is, not until now. And still they kept their thoughts to themselves. They did not want words to disturb this holy silence.

Weeks went by and it was Chanukah, the 25th day of Kislev, 5701 (1940). Dovid and Leah were returning from the Chanukah party at the *shul*. Dovid and the choir had sung his duet, but it was really Leah who sang it with him, although only from the audience. All week there was news about the war, and rumors that the Jews would soon be rounded up and put into a ghetto, or worse, sent to work camps. Everyone tried to find out what was going to happen, what they must do to save their families, their children. And still, at Chanukah, the Jews gathered to light the *menorah*, recite the blessing, and sing the songs of hope and miracle, praying with fervor, *"Not by might, nor by power, but by My spirit alone shall we all live in peace."* This was a time when those words from Zacharias, and the story of Chanukah, meant even more to every Jew.

By the end of the festival, Dovid and Leah had learned that they would be separated, for they were to go into hiding with their own families. Who knew when or how they would ever meet again? They knew, though, that their love for each other would continue.

The day after Chanukah they met to talk, perhaps for the last time. Dovid picked up his wooden and brass *menorah* and said, "Leahle, I will cut this *menorah* in half. You take one half and I'll take the other. Let's keep our halves with us always, to remind us of our love that was kindled at the beginning of this *yom tov*. Let's hope and pray, *tiere* Leahle, that we can see each other soon again in freedom and peace. Then we can sing our duet as we light our candles together as husband and wife." Leah pledged her love to Dovid, and he cut the *menorah* in half, giving one half to Leah and keeping the other for himself.

Soon after, the war came, and Leah and her family fled to Russia. All during the war Leah kept the half-*menorah* in her pocket, and when she looked at it, she felt the closeness to Dovid. All this time she did not hear any news from him. Still, she dreamed of meeting Dovid— she didn't know how or where—and of bringing the two halves of the *menorah* together. Maybe next Chanukah, she secretly hoped.

Leah often sang, but not the joyous songs that Dovid wrote, only the plaintive songs of the Jewish people. And especially when she felt loneliness or despair, she sang "*Dovdl, du lebst in mayn zikorn*. Dovidl, you live in my memory."

Dovid and his parents fought with the Partisans throughout the war. He, too, kept the *menorah* in his pocket, always checking to make sure it had not dropped out as he ran through the forests to escape from the enemy. Every time he touched it, he felt renewed courage and hope.

Finally the war was over. Joining thousands of other

Jewish survivors, Dovid and his parents walked across Europe, across snow-filled mountains and steep rocky paths, on their way to Italy. It was April 1946. When they arrived at a small port in Italy, the immigrants found a ship, hired by the Mossad emissaries, waiting for them. They crowded onto the ship and sailed to Milan. Then the immigrants, each supplied with false papers, food, and clothing, waited until dark. Using British Army vehicles as a front, they were driven to some dark, secret inlet on the Mediterranean where a boat was waiting to take them to the Land of Israel.

By dawn, the ship was on its way to the east, with the Jewish flag flying from the mast and the Jews on board singing *Hatikva*, first in Yiddish and then in Hebrew.

After a day at sea, Dovid's heart began to feel new life. He often sang for the people on the ship, songs in Yiddish, but also many Hebrew songs he had learned, with Leah, as part of the Zionist Youth Movement. He sang "Song of the Sea." He was traveling to a new land, his people's land, to a place where he didn't know what would happen, but where he could begin fresh. The first thing he would do when he arrived would be to give himself a new name, a new *mazal*. He knew the name he would choose, Uri, light. He carried always within his heart Leah's fire, and, in his pocket, his half of the *menorah*. That he would not leave behind.

It was a time when the British ruled Palestine. They patrolled the Haifa shore with boats and guns, knowing that illegal Jewish immigrants were attempting to arrive. But all this did not discourage the Jews from trying, and they were successful many times over. The landings always had to be carried out at night, with no lights so as

not to give the British any cause for suspicion. On shore, Ze'ev Hayam, the first Jewish naval captain, organized the rescue parties. The Haganah agents maintained radio contact with the refugee boat and guided it to the safest place, especially to avoid British patrols. Ze'ev Hayam waited for word that the ship had arrived, and which spot had been picked for taking the passengers from the ship. Then he signaled his men to begin the rescue. All the people held their breath hoping that the British would not be alerted and drive the ship back to Europe. The people on the boat also prayed that they would land safely on the shores of Haifa and not have to spend even more miserable days on that boat to return . . . to what?

It was quiet, except for the sound of the waves of the sea. The signal came at last. The waiting men began to move, and like a choreographed dance, they walked into the waters of Bat Galim, toward the boat. They walked into the water up to their chins, forming a man-made bridge of shoulders. Then the people left the boat and walked on these men's shoulders until they reached the shallow waters and the sandy beach, the land. Women and men, doctors and nurses, were waiting there, each one taking someone, a man or woman or child who had just come from the boat. Quietly, quickly, they whisked them away, smuggling them to their homes.

The next day, the British began looking for the people from the boat. No one knew anything about them. "Of course not. People landing at Bat Galim? Really? That's not possible. No, I haven't seen anyone. I was home asleep."

After a few days, the Jews from Europe were rested, received a new set of false papers and new clothes and

100

were then reunited with their families. Dovid, or rather Uri, was reunited with his parents and they began to make a new life for themselves, not only learning the language, adjusting to the new climate, and meeting new people, but also seeking out their *landsleit* from Eastern Europe.

Uri searched everywhere and asked everyone he met about Leah. He followed every lead he heard about. But no one knew anything. Some people tried to give him hope that he would find her. Others just shrugged their shoulders and lowered their eyes, not saying a word. Everyone was looking for a loved one. Survivors were scattered all over the world.

All this time Uri was becoming an Israeli. He learned to speak Hebrew, he attended school, he fought in the War of Independence, and then decided to become a cantor. He loved Haifa, his first home in the Jewish state. As he walked down and up the hills, he could smell the beautiful fragrance of jasmine. He would look and see everywhere the stately cedars and graceful cypresses. But he saw them through a veil of tears as he recited, "'*The beams of our house are cedar, cypresses are our rafters.*' Oh, Leahle, oh, my beloved." And Uri would quickly run to a place where he could weep for his beloved Leah in solitude.

Uri often sang for the people at the old age home, especially the songs in Yiddish that they remembered. Hearing those songs helped bring them closer to their homes, to the people they remembered, to the life that was never to be again. They lived with their memories and they loved the sweet voice of their cantor. The home was on the Carmel, looking down on Bat Galim, the beach where Uri had first arrived in Israel.

He started visiting the people there just before Rosh
Hashanah that year, 1948, when Israel became a State. It
was a strange little lady he met at the synagogue who
brought him there. She said to him, "Cantor, we need to
hear those songs to keep the spark of our Jewishness
alive. Come sing for us." She sat there that first day,
wearing a bonnet and wrapped in a large flowered shawl
and smiling all the while as he sang. And though he went
there at least once a week, he never saw her there again.
When he asked about her, no one seemed to know her. It
was as if she had disappeared into thin air.

It was Chanukah in Israel. Uri was on the way to the
old age home to help the people there celebrate the *yom
tov* by chanting the blessings over the first candle and
singing a concert of holiday songs. As he was crossing the
little crooked street, he looked up at the star-filled sky,
remembering another first night of Chanukah, and then
he saw something in a window. He thought perhaps he
was still retaining the image of the stars and he blinked
hard and looked again. He thought he saw half a *menorah*
made of wood and brass. He must be imagining it, he
thought. Perhaps the curtain was draped over the other
half. There was one candle lit in it, but after all it was
hard to see what it really was when it was so dark.

That night, Uri could not sleep well. He dreamed that
he was there with Leah, in his house, playing the piano
and singing *Haneiros Halalu.* He had not sung that duet
since they had had to part, since the night he separated
the *menorah* in half.

In the morning, he woke with a start. "Should I perhaps go to that house and ask, 'How did you get that
half-*menorah?*' They'll think I'm crazy. 'Half-*menorah*,

Cantor? No one lights only half a *menorah*.'" All day long, Uri was in a daze. He could not concentrate on his work. He went to the synagogue, but did not know what he was doing. Finally, he was determined to go back that night, to pass the house again, and see whether what he had noticed the night before was really there. If not, then he would know that he had imagined it. They say that if you really want to see something, it will appear. The mind can play tricks.

That day seemed to last a thousand hours. Finally, it was almost dark. He walked slowly to that street. He kept from looking at the stars. Instead he looked directly up at the window. It was there, but this time with two candles. He stood there frozen, his mind wanting to believe, to hope, but . . . what if he were to be disappointed? Maybe someone had found the *menorah*. . . . He stopped thinking about it, and knocked on the door. The door was slightly ajar. A woman's voice called out in Hebrew, "*Yavo*—Come in."

It is the voice of my beloved, thought Uri. Without thinking, yet not wanting to scare her, he began to sing softly the first line, "*Haneiros halalu onu madlikin*." Then he stopped, and just as softly her voice echoed back, "*Haneiros halalu onu madlikin*."

All during the week of Chanukah, Uri and Leah talked about what had happened to them since their last time together. But at times they shared only silence between them. Leah spoke about the years in Russia and how she and her family, at the end of the war, arrived in Israel with the help of the Jewish Agency. Then she added, in a teasing voice, "You may have come by ship to Eretz Yisrael, Dovidl, but we came by an underground

railroad, which I helped dig with my half of the *menorah.*"

"Well, I helped row the ship with my half of the *menorah,*" Dovid retorted. And they both laughed in a way that they had not in years.

Suddenly Leah stopped laughing and said quietly, "Dovid, I've just had a strange memory. I just remembered an old woman who was with us as we left Russia. One day, as we were walking through a village, my part of the *menorah* dropped from my pocket. This woman—I don't even know her name. All I recall is that she wore a wonderful large shawl and she had a smile that filled my heart with hope—picked up the *menorah.* As she handed it back to me, she said, almost like a blessing, "You will find your destined love in Israel." I wonder who she was and where she is now. I would like to thank her and invite her to our wedding."

"Was it a big, *flowered* shawl?" asked Dovid.

"Yes," answered Leah with surprise. "How did you know that?"

Dovid gave Leah a hug and danced with her around the room, singing loudly and laughing, at the same time.

"Dovid! Dovid! What is it? Do you know this woman? Tell me, Dovid, how you knew she wore a flowered shawl," Leah demanded. But Dovid kept singing and dancing without answering.

Finally, out of breath, he said, "Leahle, that old woman was Sarah Bat Tuvim. I'm sure of it. The woman you met and the woman who invited me to sing at the old age home are the same woman. It was Sarah Bat Tuvim. Don't you remember reading about her in folk tales when we were children? She helps arrange marriages, a

104

sort of *shadchente*, who also had a habit of vanishing. And it was she who brought us together in Israel."

Uri and Leah, who decided to call herself Orah, which also means light, got married on the eighth night of Chanukah. Uri brought to the wedding his half of the *menorah*. Orah brought her half also. This was the gift they gave to each other. For the first time since that night so long ago, they lit the candles on their *menorah*, fitted together to make it whole, and sang the blessings, adding the *shehecheyanu*. Then the beloveds began to sing *Haneiros Halalu*, their voices weaving together the joy they were feeling in their hearts. As they were singing, Orah and Uri looked out at a table near the door. One woman was sitting there, alone. She was wearing a flowered shawl and a bonnet—and she was smiling.

HANEIROS HALOLU הנרות הללו

107

From *Kol Rinah Utfilah*; composed by Cantor S. E. Manchester 1942

DOVIDL

An unpublished song by popular Yiddish folk poet
Mordecai Gebirtig (1877–1942) killed by the Nazis. The
text is from a manuscript in the YIVO Archives. Gebirtig
was the author of many song favorites like "*Reyzele*,"
"*Yankele*," "*Moyshele, mayn fraynd*" (Moyshele, my
friend), "*Dray tekhterlekh*" (Three daughters).

Dovidl, er lebt in mayn zikorn,
Un khotsh er iz avek fun mir shoyn lang,
Ze ikh im nokh in zayne kinderyorn,
Klingt nokh zayn kol mir vi a zis gezang.

Refrain:
Dovidl, gedenkstu nokh,
Mir zaynen beyde kinderlekh geven?
Dovidl, tsi benkstu nokh,
Tsi hostu ven in kholem mikh gezen?
Dovidl, gedenkstu nokh
Dos alte hayzl, di kleyne shtiblekh tsvey,
Gut iz mir
Geven a mol mit dir,
Ven beyde hobn mir
Gevoynt in zey;
Gut iz mir
Geven a mol mit dir,
Itst bistu vayt fun mir,
Alts geyt farbay.

Dovidl, mir shpiln zikh tsuzamen,
Ot zaynen mir nokh yunge kinder tsvey,
Un s'kvelt mayn mame, shmeykhlt tsu
        zayn mamen,—
S'vet a sheyn porl zayn a mol fun zey.

דודל, ער לעבט אין מײַן זיכּרון,
און כאָטש ער איז אַוועק פֿון מיר שױן לאַנג,
זע איך אים נאָך אין זײַנע קינדעריאָרן,
קלינגט נאָך זײַן קול מיר װי אַ זיס געזאַנג.

רעפֿרײַן:
דודל, געדענקסטו נאָך,
מיר זײַנען ביידע קינדערלעך געװוען?
דודל, צי בענקסטו נאָך,
צי האָסטו װען אין חלום מיך געזען?
דודל, געדענקסטו נאָך
דאָס אַלטע הײַזל, די קליינע שטיבלעך צװיי?
גוט איז מיר
געװוען אַ מאָל מיט דיר,
װען ביידע האָבן מיר
געװוינט אין זיי;
גוט איז מיר
געװוען אַ מאָל מיט דיר,
איצט ביסטו װײַט פֿון מיר,
אַלץ גייט פֿאַרבײַ.

דודל, מיר שפּילן זיך צוזאַמען,
אָט זײַנען מיר נאָך יונגע קינדער צװיי,
און ס'קװועלט מײַן מאַמע, שמייכלט צו
        זײַן מאַמען, —
ס'װועט אַ שיין פּאָרל זײַן אַ מאָל פֿון זיי.

110

Refrain:
Dovidl, gedenkstu nokh. . .

רעפֿריין:
דודל, געדענקסטו נאָך. . .

Dovidl, shoyn shpeter a sakh yorn
Iz vayt avek, bashert mir nisht geven,
Mayn mames vuntsh mekuyem nisht gevorn,
Avek un mer im keyn mol nisht gezen.

דודל, שוין שפּעטער אַ סך יאָרן,
איז ווײַט אַוועק, באַשערט מיר נישט געווען,
מײַן מאַמעס ווונטש ווונטש מקוים נישט געוואָרן,
אַוועק און מער אים קיין מאָל נישט געזען.

Dovidl, gedenkstu nokh
Di letste nakht, dem letstn 'blayb
    gezunt'?
Dovidl, zint yene nakht
Geblibn iz in hartsn mir a vund,
Dovidl, gedenkstu nokh,
Du host geshvoyrn vest eybik zayn
    mir tray?
Gut iz mir
Geven a mol mit dir,
Flegst brengen blimlekh mir,
Kh'benk haynt nokh zey.
Gut iz mir
Geven a mol mit dir,
Un itst dos harts zogt mir,
Iz alts farbay.

דודל, געדענקסטו נאָך
די לעצטע נאַכט, דעם לעצטן ׳בלײַב
    געזונט׳?
דודל, זינט יענע נאַכט
געבליבן איז אין האַרצן מיר אַ וווּנד,
דודל, געדענקסטו נאָך,
דו האָסט געשוווירן וועסט אייביק זײַן
    מיר טרײַ?
גוט איז מיר
געווען אַ מאָל מיט דיר,
פֿלעגסט ברענגען בלימלעך מיר,
כ׳בענק הײַנט נאָך זיי.
גוט איז מיר
געווען אַ מאָל מיט דיר,
און איצט דאָס האַרץ זאָגט מיר,
איז אַלץ פֿאַרבײַ.

Dovidl, he lives in my memory, and though he went away from me so long ago, I can still see how he looked when he was a child, I can still hear his sweet voice. Dovidl, do you remember when we were both children? Do you miss me, dream of me? Dovidl, do you remember the old house, the two small rooms? How good it was to be with you when we lived there! Now you're far away. Everything passes.

Dovidl, we're playing together. We're still children. And my mother glows with pride and smiles to his mother that one day we would be a good match. So many years passed and it wasn't destined. My mother's wish did not come true. He went away and I never saw him again.

Dovidl, do you remember the last night we spent together, the last 'farewell'? Since that night a wound remained in my heart. Do you remember that you swore that you would always be true to me? How good it was to be with you! You would bring me flowers; I still long for them. And now my heart tells me that all is over.

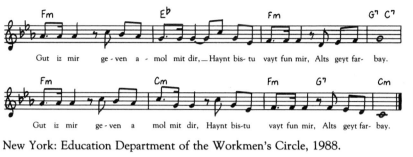

Gut iz mir ge-ven a-mol mit dir,—Haynt bis-tu vayt fun mir, Alts geyt far- bay.

Gut iz mir ge-ven a mol mit dir, Haynt bis-tu vayt fun mir, Alts geyt far- bay.

New York: Education Department of the Workmen's Circle, 1988.

YAM-LID
Song Of The Sea

Hebrew words by the poet Judah ha-Levi (1075?–1141). Translated into Yiddish by Chaim Nachman Bialik (1873–1934). The music by M. Shneyer (1885–1942) was published by Jos. P. Katz, N.Y. in 1917.

Kh'hob fargesn ale libste,
Kh'hob farlozt mayn eygn hoyz;
Kh'hob dem yam zikh opgegebn;
Trog mikh, yam, tsum muters shoys.

כ׳האָב פֿאַרגעסן אַלע ליבסטע,
כ׳האָב פֿאַרלאָזט מײַן אײגן הויז;
כ׳האָב דעם ים זיך אָפּגעגעבן:
טראָג מיך, ים, צום מוטערס שויס.

Refrain:
Un du, mayrev-vint getrayer,
Trayb mayn shif tsu yenem breg,
Vos mayn harts mit odler-fligl
Zukht shoyn lang tsu im a veg.

רעפֿריין:
און דו, מערבֿ־ווינט געטרײַער,
טרײַב מײַן שיף צו יענעם ברעג,
וואָס מײַן האַרץ מיט אָדלער־פֿליגל
זוכט שוין לאַנג צו אים אַ וועג.

Breng mikh nor ahin besholem,—
Nokh dem fli zikh dir tsurik,
Grisn zolstu ale libste
Un dertseyl zey fun mayn glik.

ברענג מיך נאָר אַהין בשלום,—
נאָך דעם פֿלי זיך דיר צוריק,
גריסן זאָלסטו אַלע ליבסטע
און דערצייל זיי פֿון מײַן גליק.

113

I have forgotten all my loved ones, I have left my own home. I've abandoned myself to the sea: carry me, Sea, to my mother's bosom!

And you, loyal West Wind, drive my ship to that shore, where my heart on eagle's wings has long been seeking a path.

Bring me there unharmed and then fly back again. Give greetings to all my loved ones and tell them of my happiness.

New York: Education Department of the Workmen's Circle, 1988.

114

-DIE HOFFENUNG (HATIKVOH)

In Yiddish דִי הָאָפֿענונג (התקוה)

Main folk ich kum dir treistn hob

hoffenung un mut dain hilf main folk vet kumen dir vet zein noch gut dein

cholem dem zi senfun nviem pro fetzait du verst bef raitfun tfi se

From *Kol Rinah Utfilah*

116

1.

Mein folk ich kum dir treisten
  hob hoffenung und muth
Dein hilf mein folk vet kumen
  dir vet zein noch gut
Dein cholem dem zisen
  fun neviem proftzeit
Du verst befreit fun t'fiseh
  dein g'uloh is nit veit

Refrain:

Kom flakert noch die zehnzucht
  in dos yidish hertz
Und beinkt noch alts noch zion
  mit weimuth und mit shmerts
Kom vendet noch der yid
  tzu mizroch zu zein blik
Dan lebt noch die hoffenung
  zein tzukunft und zein glik

2.

Es molt mir mein fantasye
  bilder ohn a tzohl
Ich zeh mein folk yisroel
  lebt gliklich vie a mohl
Er lebt a freies leben
  in zein eigenes land
Keiner reibt zein kovoid
  men macht ihm nit zu shand

Refrain:

3.

Es rufen berg und tohlen
  der himmel winkt zu dir

מיין פֿאָלק איך קום דיר טרייסטען
האָב האָפּפּענונג און מוטה
דיין הילף מיין פֿאָלק וועט קומען
דיר וועט זיין נאָך גוט
דיין חלום דעם זיסען
פֿון נביאים פּראָפֿעצייהט
דו ווערסט בפֿרייט פֿון תפֿיסה
דיין גאולה איז ניט ווייט

כאָרוס . . .

קומס פֿלאָקערט נאָך די זעהנזוכט
אין דאָס אידיש הערץ
און ביינקט נאָך אַלץ נאָך ציון
מיט וועהמוטה און מיט שמערץ
קומס ווענדעט נאָך דער איד
צו מזרח צו זיין בליק
דאַן לעבט נאָך די האָפּפּענונג
זיין צוקונפֿט און זיין גליק.

2.

עס מאָהלט מיר מיין פֿאַנטאַזיע
בילדער אָהן אַ צאָהל
איך זעה מיין פֿאָלק ישראל
לעבט גליקליך ווי אַמאָהל
ער לעבט אַ פֿרייעם לעבען
אין זיין אייגענעם לאַנד
קיינער רויבט זיין כבוד
מען מאַכט איהם ניט צו שאַנד

כאָרוס . . .

3.

עס רופֿען בערג און טהאָלען
דער הימעל ווינקט צו דיר

117

Es ruft der har hashoron
   yisroel kum zu mir
Darum mein folk yisroel
   zu zion vend dein blik
Nor dort gefinstu ruhe
   nor dorten ruht dein glik
Refrain:

עס רופט דער הר השרון
ישראל קום צו מיר
דאַרום מיין פאָלק ישראל
צו ציון ווענד דיין בליק
נור דאָרט געפינסטו רוהע
נור דאָרטען רוהט דיין גליק.
כאָרוס . . .

HATIKVA

Kol od baleyvav p'nimah
Nefesh y'hudi homiah
Ulfa-atei mizrach kadimah
Ayin l'tzion tzofiah
Od lo avda tikvateynu
Hatikva (bat) sh'not alpayim
Lih'yot am chofshi b'artzeynu
Eretz tzion virushalayim.

כָּל־עוֹד בַּלֵּבָב פְּנִימָה
נֶפֶשׁ יְהוּדִי הוֹמִיָּה
וּלְפַאֲתֵי מִזְרָח קָדִימָה
עַיִן לְצִיּוֹן צוֹפִיָּה.
עוֹד לֹא אָבְדָה תִּקְוָתֵנוּ
הַתִּקְוָה בַּת שְׁנוֹת אַלְפַּיִם
לִהְיוֹת עַם חָפְשִׁי בְּאַרְצֵנוּ
אֶרֶץ צִיּוֹן וִירוּשָׁלָיִם.

As long as a Jewish heart beats,
And as long as Jewish eyes look eastwards,
Then our two thousand year hope
To be a free nation in Zion
Is not lost.

Hebrew text by N. H. Imber

Appendix 1

Music for Chanukah Blessings

HANUKAH BLESSINGS

(From Traditional tunes)
Edited RJN

Ba - ruh a-ta a-do-nai e-lo - hé-nu me-leh ha-o-lam a - sher kid-sha-nu b'-mits-vo-

-tav v'-tsi - va-nu l'-had-lik nér shel ha-nu-ka ba-ruh a-ta a-do-nai e-lo-

-hé-nu me-leh ha-o-lam she-a - sa ni-sim she-a-sa ni-sim she-a-

-sa ni-sim laavo-té-nu she-a-sa ni-sim she-a-sa ni-sim she-a-

-sa ni-sim la a vo-té-nu she-a - sa ni-sim la-a-vo-té-

-nu ba-ya-mim ha - hém baz'-man ha-ze.

בָּרוּךְ אַתָּה יְיָ אֱלֹהֵינוּ מֶלֶךְ הָעוֹלָם אֲשֶׁר
קִדְּשָׁנוּ בְּמִצְוֹתָיו וְצִוָּנוּ לְהַדְלִיק נֵר שֶׁל חֲנֻכָּה.
בָּרוּךְ אַתָּה יְיָ אֱלֹהֵינוּ מֶלֶךְ הָעוֹלָם שֶׁעָשָׂה נִסִּים
לַאֲבוֹתֵינוּ בַּיָּמִים הָהֵם בַּזְּמַן הַזֶּה.

121

HANEROT HALALU

Hassidic
Arr. R. J. Neumann

122

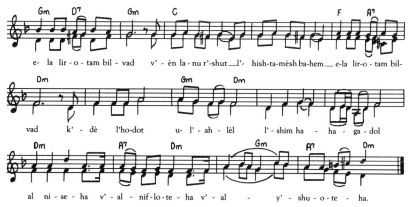

e - la li - ro - tam bil - vad v' - én la - nu r'-shut l' hish-ta-mésh ba-hem — e-la li-ro - tam bil-

vad k'- dé l'ho-dot u- l'- ah- lél l'- shim ha - ha- ga - dol

al ni- se- ha v'- al- nif-lo-te- ha v'- al y'- shu- o- te- ha.

From *Hanukah Melodies*. Cedarhurst, NY: Board of Jewish Education of Greater New York and Tara Publications, 1977.

הַנֵּרוֹת הַלָּלוּ אֲנַחְנוּ מַדְלִיקִים עַל הַנִּסִּים וְעַל הַנִּפְלָאוֹת וְעַל הַתְּשׁוּעוֹת וְעַל הַמִּלְחָמוֹת שֶׁעָשִׂיתָ
לַאֲבוֹתֵינוּ בַּיָּמִים הָהֵם בַּזְּמַן הַזֶּה עַל יְדֵי כֹּהֲנֶיךָ הַקְּדוֹשִׁים. וְכָל שְׁמוֹנַת יְמֵי חֲנֻכָּה הַנֵּרוֹת הַלָּלוּ
קֹדֶשׁ הֵם וְאֵין לָנוּ רְשׁוּת לְהִשְׁתַּמֵּשׁ בָּהֶם אֶלָּא לִרְאוֹתָם בִּלְבָד כְּדֵי לְהוֹדוֹת וּלְהַלֵּל לְשִׁמְךָ הַגָּדוֹל
עַל נִסֶּיךָ וְעַל יְשׁוּעָתֶךָ וְעַל נִפְלְאוֹתֶיךָ

BLESSING FOR CHANUKAH

Freely

Ba - ruch a - ta A - do - nai E - lo -

he - nu mel-lech ha - o - lam a - sher ki-d'- sha-nu b'- mitz-vo-tav v'- tzi -

va - nu l'- had - lik ner shel Cha-nu-ka

From *Sephardic Songs of Praise*, ed. A. L. Cardozo. Cedarhurst, NY: Tara Publications, 1987.

123

Blessed are You, Lord our God,
Ruler of the universe. You
have sanctified us with Your
commandments and ordained
that we kindle the Canukah
lights.

בָּרוּךְ אַתָּה יְיָ
אֱלֹהֵינוּ מֶלֶךְ הָעוֹלָם
אֲשֶׁר קִדְּשָׁנוּ בְּמִצְוֹתָיו
וְצִוָּנוּ לְהַדְלִיק נֵר שֶׁל חֲנֻכָּה

HANEROT HALALU

The Western Sephardim use oil lights exclusively for
lighting the Chanukah lamp, the *menorah*. After the
blessings, the *Hanerot Halalu* is sung.

From *Sephardic Songs of Praise*, ed. A. L. Cardozo. Cedarhurst, NY: Tara Publications, 1987.

We light these lights on
Account of the marvelous
Liberation, and the strength,
The wonder and the comforts.

הַנֵּרוֹת הַלָּלוּ אָנוּ מַדְלִיקִין
עַל הַנִּסִּים וְעַל הַפֻּרְקָן
וְעַל הַגְּבוּרוֹת
וְעַל הַתְּשׁוּעוֹת
וְעַל הַנִּפְלָאוֹת
וְעַל הַנֶּחָמוֹת

BIRCHATH CHANUKOH ברכות חנוכה

125

From *Kol Rinah Utfilah*; composed by Cantor S. E. Manchester 1942

Appendix 2

Retrieving Family Stories

We all love a good story, and through tales and legends the history, religion, holidays, and values of a nation and a people live on. Jews are a storytelling people and our diverse and vibrant tales reflect the Jewish experience from every corner of the world. Storytelling has been—and remains—the traditional method of transmitting the Jewish religious and cultural heritage through oral expression. Storytelling has served as a form of entertainment, but even more, as a form of social and moral instruction presented in creative and fanciful ways. The lesson is learned better when it is also pleasing.

For the Jew, storytelling has always been a way to transmit Jewish learning, traditions, customs, laws, and values from one generation to the next. As Jews traveled from country to country and settled in many lands, they learned to speak the language of the land as well as that of the Jews in that land, and adopted different modes of

129

dress, too. However, they continued to pray in the sacred Hebrew language and to cling to their main unifying idea of one God. They studied and shared the stories of the Jewish People which they carried with them and which they learned from traveling rabbis (*maggidim, badchanim*) and messengers. The stories created a bond among Jews everywhere.

Because it has remained an integral part of Jewish religion and society, storytelling in Jewish life continues to be an ongoing, effective way of transmitting a cultural heritage and thereby of sharing the values of a people. Jewish storytellers (including parents, educators, and rabbis) draw their material from a culture rich in Bible stories, the narratives in rabbinic literature (e.g., parables, *midrashim*, and fables), folktales, myths, fairytales, proverbs, anecdotes, and legends.

The oral tradition pertains primarily to the accumulated folklore, legends, sayings, and customs of the Jewish People that are handed down by word of mouth. It stresses the human connection between a parent/teacher/storyteller and the child/student/listener in transmitting stories. In addition to the wealth of new interpretations from every age, the oral tradition preserves the various styles of telling and the different versions of stories.

When they hear a good story, Jewish storytellers will transform that story into a Jewish tale. This transformation has happened throughout the ages and in many countries since Jews have lived in many parts of the world and have spoken the languages of many countries. Thus, we find many Jewish stories and themes in our literature and oral tradition that originated in, for example, Arabic literature or Russian literature. But, of course, the reverse is true, too. That is how many rabbinic stories found their way into *The Arabian Nights*. This can be called the fluid folklore process, and it explains why there are variants of many stories found all over the world. The oral tradition weaves the threads of many traditions, customs, laws, ethics and imagination into folktales, legends, and *midrashim*, parables, fables, sayings, and riddles.

Among the Jewish people, storytelling is a dynamic experience that occurs both in the synagogue and in the home. However, there are distinctions among the varied oral narrative activities in Jewish life. There is the oral reading of stories from the Torah in a liturgical setting, as well as the reading of the *Megillah* on the holiday of Purim, also in the synagogue; there is the oral reading of the story of the Exodus around the dinner table at home on Passover; and there are stories created imaginatively by the parent and others in the home, such as the recounting of family stories in one's own words, or the retelling of existing stories and legends from books or from memory.

Jews tell stories all the time. Every holiday, and there are many, offers an opportunity for storytelling, both in the home and in the synagogue. Holidays are celebrations of our memories, a time to connect us with the past in order to remember and to live wisely now and in the future, a time to keep alive our people and our traditions, customs, and values, a time to be thankful, a time to be open to a sense of wonder, a time to tell stories. Chanukah is such a time!

The magical "I'm going to tell you a story" around the Sabbath table, the Chanukah table, or at any time creates a willingness to listen and a desire to know, to participate. When a storyteller tells a story, something special happens. With each story, the listener takes a journey to distant lands (especially to the Land of Israel), meets new characters, understands new ideas, discovers options and, most of all, absorbs the values of Judaism. Jewish values, such as learning Torah, peoplehood, the Sabbath, family, *tzedakah*, and freedom, are folk values in that they reflect collective, rather than individual judgments. Within the diversity of Jewish stories, these values continue to evolve and remain meaningful to the Jew today.

Sitting around the table after a Friday or holiday meal, parents might exchange experiences they had had in their life or tell legends. The pictures and sounds formed in the mind at such a time stay with the child. These become shared experiences, stories that serve as a link in the passing time between generations, between human beings of another country and time and you and the teller of the story, today. We relive through our imaginations what they experienced. We smell the bread making or the potato *kugel* baking; we touch the velvet of a special dress; we see the wonders of the marketplace; we hear the wagon drivers shouting; we cry, we laugh—together. We celebrate together. We know we are part of the human race and part of the Jewish People.

A good story triggers a memory, a sense memory or a situation memory, which leads to someone telling another story. No doubt you yourself have said or heard someone say, "That reminds me of a story," or "That reminds me of a similar story," or "Listen to this one!" Sometimes the story is a family or personal remembrance, and other times it is a folktale or traditional story. Sometimes what we think is a personal/family story is really a folktale handed down through the generations, but in the journey it has become more and more personalized.

In the next section are two memory stories by the book's authors that echo a fascinating custom among some Jewish communities. In certain Sephardi cities, two *shammash* lights were kindled in the *chanukiot*, one to commemorate the miracle of Chanukah, the other to commemorate deliverance from local persecution. In Eastern Europe, in order to have better balance, aesthetically and for hanging on the wall when not in use, many of the bench-type Chanukah lamps had two sockets for the *shammash* instead of one. Just as in our book the story of Chanukah serves as the first *shammash* to lead our readers into the stories for each night, so we offer these two memory stories as a second *shammash* reflecting this interesting tradition as a spur for the telling of your own stories.

Memories are the keys that unlock the many stories we carry within us. We all have lots of story-producing memories—memories to be retrieved, activated, and kept alive as stories. The following series of exercises will help you find your personal and family Chanukah stories which you can then tell, and retell, each year during the eight nights and eight days of the holiday.

Places

The memory of a place often brings with it memories of events. To retrieve the stories that happened in a particular location, we must mentally move back to that place and time—the setting acts as a "hook" to pull the story from its hidden places.

1. Recreate the place where you lit the Chanukah *menorah*. On what was the *menorah* standing? Describe that piece of furniture.

2. Recreate other rooms in the house where the holiday celebration took place: the kitchen where the *latkes* or other special holiday foods were cooked, the dining room, the pantry or cellar where the potatoes and other foods were kept, the place where the *dreidle* game was played, and so forth.

People

Making characters come to life will bring success to your stories—personal or traditional. Choose people in your life and describe them, bringing them alive through details such as mannerisms, clothing, favorite phrases, favorite topics of conversation, posture, hobbies, place at the table, specific facial expressions, favorite jokes/songs/quotes. When you describe these people use nouns as well as adjectives to convey the essence of the characters (animate and inanimate). What roles did they play in life? Who sang the Chanukah blessings and songs? Who was the storyteller in the family? Who gave out the Chanukah *gelt* or other presents?

Objects and Photographs

Objects that we possess or remember can often trigger a story. Thus, you can help uncover these stories by asking yourself: What object(s) do I have that reminds me of Chanukah—a *menorah*, a particular piece of jewelry or gift given to me at Chanukah, a *dreidle*, a recipe for potato *latkes* or other special holiday foods, photographs taken during Chanukah? How did you obtain this object? Where did your *menorah* come from originally? Describe the objects you have or that you recall from another time.

Proverbs, Folk Sayings, Advice, and Songs

Chances are, your parents and grandparents had a particular set of proverbs, folk sayings, songs, and advice that crept into their conversations, especially during a holiday; for example, one such folk belief is watching the candles until they burn out so you don't shame them. The various Chanukah songs in Yiddish, Hebrew, Ladino, and so forth become your family songs. Try to remember them, or find them in the various song anthologies that are available.

Smells and Sights

Marcel Proust took advantage of the fact that the sense of smell often serves as a springboard to memory. Some

135

studies have concluded that of all the senses, smell triggers the most vivid memories. Think of certain smells that bring back a memory: the smell of potato *latkes* or jelly doughnuts frying or the colorful little Chanukah candles burning in the *menorah*. Recreate the scene that involved these smells and sights.

Experiences

What was the happiest Chanukah you can remember? The funniest episode during Chanukah? The most poignant moment? The best gift you ever gave or received at this holiday? A special visit? These are trigger phrases to start you off on some high points, but they might also remind you of those tinier moments that are just as important in shaping lives and relationships.

All these personal and family stories, traditional tales, and folk sayings have enriched the life of the Jewish People and helped the individual live the life of a Jew. They also create in all of us a need to continue the tradition of "planting" stories in the minds and hearts of our next generation. A storytelling approach makes our heritage, holidays, and history vital because it gives them a context, a rich pudding of plot and character that illustrates the times. When a generation can feel its ancestors' feelings and share their ideas and sorrows, the lessons in their lives will live on in the next generation. The Torah associates wisdom with the heart, and not with the mind. So it is to the heart we must direct our stories, where truth and wisdom can be found by those who care to listen. There is always a time for telling stories in Jewish

136

life—and there is always a story to fit the time. Storytelling not only reflects Jewish life, it perpetuates it.

By telling and retelling all of our stories, we bring more light to the holiday, we help to increase and spread this holy light to our children and friends, we help create something beautiful, and we continue to give thanks and praise God's name for God's miracles, wonders, and deliverances—*Haneirot Halalu.*

Happy Chanukah!

Appendix 3

The Second Shammash:
Two Chanukah Memories

THE SUBSTITUTE SHAMMAS

Peninnah Schram

"Papa, what are you doing with the *menorah*?" I asked.

"The *shammas* holder broke off and I can't find it. So I'm replacing it. After all, a Chanukah *menorah* is not a Chanukah *menorah* without a proper *shammas*. It'll be as good as new," assured my father after he had seen my worried, uncertain look. I knew my father to be clever, but not a craftsman. "And," continued my father, "tonight we'll light the first candle, eat *latkes* and I'll tell you the story of Chanukah."

And that night, as Papa had promised, we lit the first candle, ate *latkes*, even drank glasses of tea with that delicious cherry jelly my mother always prepared, and, yes, he told me the story of Chanukah, as he did every year. And, yes, the *menorah* may have been repaired, but

it certainly was not new. My father had brought it with him when he came to America from Lithuania at the turn of the century. It was over forty years old. It was a heavy metal *menorah* with eight metal cups to be filled with oil for lighting; there were tiny covers for each cup. The high metal back was impressive: two columns with vines wrapped around them on each side topped with metal flames. On the very top, in the center, was a cut-out crown. In the middle of the back plate were two lions on either side of a seven-branched *menorah*, each lion holding onto it with one paw, and each looking up at it. To me it seemed like a theatrical backdrop for the drama of the little flames. Oh, yes. At the top of the right-hand column, but just below the metal flame, was placed the *shammas* cup, which was now replaced by a long, deeper oblong cup-like metal piece and attached to the *menorah* with a bent piece of stiff wire. Oh, how ingenious my father was, I thought to myself.

Chanukah was such a joyous time in our home! To be given the *shammas* to light the first candle while we sang the blessings was a special treat. Then we would watch the dancing lights while we ate *latkes* and sang more songs. During that half hour or so, my father would also tell me about the Maccabees and their fight for freedom. He would explain why we Jews celebrate this holiday with light and song and thanksgiving.

Only after the candles had gone out would we go off to the *shul* for a community Chanukah celebration. The women of the Ladies Auxiliary of the synagogue were all busy frying hundreds of *latkes* in the big synagogue kitchen and serving them on the long tables where families sat and socialized. There was some kind of entertainment along with the cantor, my father, singing cantorial and Yiddish songs. But what I waited for each year was when a man by the name of Mr. Harry Gordon would take his seat behind a certain small table, with shiny pennies piled up in front of him and the children all lined up as well. He would greet each child by name and ask, "How old are you this year?" And then he would give each of us Chanukah *gelt* according to our age—5 years old, five pennies; 8 years old, eight pennies; and so on. I treasured that gift as I treasure this memory.

One Chanukah many years later, after we had lit the candles, I wondered about the substitute *shammas*. I asked my father, "Where did you get this replacement for the *shammas* holder, Pa? It has certainly lasted all these years. What was it used for originally?"

"It's a bullet casing. I asked one of Mama's tenants for a suggestion for what I could use, and since he was a sailor stationed at the Submarine Base, he brought me this empty bullet shell," answered my father. "It looked like it would fit right in to serve as the *shammas* holder."

As I thought about it and observed it carefully, I suddenly said, "Papa, it's absolutely perfect that this bullet casing be on a *menorah*. After all, when the Maccabees found the Temple desecrated and the *menorah* destroyed, they used spears to hold the cruses of oil so they could dedicate the Temple. Doesn't it say in Isaiah that peace will come when we beat our swords into ploughshares? Maybe we should add, 'And our bullets into *menorahs*!'"

I now have inherited this *menorah*, the *menorah* I love, so filled with memories and lights. And when I light the *shammas* each year for the eight nights of Chanukah, it is also the *shammas* holder that holds a special meaning for me.

A MEMORY OF CHANUKAH
IN THE SUBURBS

Steven M. Rosman

My earliest memories of Chanukah place me back in the suburbs as a young child. My parents had moved me and my two younger brothers to a place "where kids have grass to play on" and "where we have our own backyard." No longer did my parents have to worry about my running into the busy streets of the Bronx, dodging cars, buses, taxis, and jaywalking pedestrians.

Chanukah in these suburbs arrived just as the other major celebrations in our lives did: when Daddy came home. From the moment I awakened in the morning, I was obsessed with the thought of his return. Eternity seemed an instant compared with the interminable wait for my father.

Then the skies would darken, the evening kiddie shows would air on TV, and we would listen for the sound of the garage door, signaling Daddy's home! When that front door opened, my brothers and I would rush to hug his pants legs, since that was as high as we could reach, and hurry him into his bedroom so that he could take off his jacket and tie and begin the festivities.

I ran to the bureau in the living room to get the prayer book. It was an old Birnbaum *Siddur*, which included blessings for holidays like Chanukah. My father kept his black *yarmulke* inserted in the prayerbook like a bookmark. It was easy to find the page for the Chanukah blessings: it was the one dotted with the melted wax that dripped from the *shammash* as my father held it aloft during his recitation. That page was a technicolor wonderland, filled with the hues of all the different colors of all the different candles that had served as our *shammash* over the years. That prayer book had been my grandfather's prayer book. Whenever my dad would hold the prayer book in one hand and the *shammash* in the other, I felt a transcendent connection to my Papa Max, as if he were hovering over us in our kitchen.

My father intoned the blessings and handed the candle to my mother. We had our own traditional protocol for kindling the Chanukah lights; my mother lit the first candle, I lit the next, since I was the eldest son, then came each of my brothers according to their ages. This *chanukiah* burned on the kitchen table. But we had an electric *chanukiah* for the window, as well. This one was kindled by tightening the bulbs in their sockets. It was always a confusing process for me. The lights were illuminated in the opposite direction from the ones on the kitchen table because they had to face the outside to proclaim to the world that here was a Jewish house. I always seemed to forget and tighten the wrong bulbs.

We lived in a part of the suburbs that was predominantly Christian. So after dinner we would all bundle up and pile into the station wagon for our annual tour of *chanukiot*. My father would drive us around our neighborhood first, and then into the more Jewish neighborhoods so that we could see all the different kinds of *window-chanukiot* and feel a bond with other Jews. My brothers and I would count the number of Jewish homes on each block, "one, two, three . . . ," and determine which block and which neighborhood had the most Jews. We never knew who lived behind the walls in those homes, but we felt a warmth and a connection to each one of them by virtue of the *chanukiah* in the window.

Even now, when I see the lights of a *chanukiah* twinkling in the night of winter, I feel a rush of warmth that permeates my whole being. Each of those flames is a glowing invitation to a memory.

Appendix 4

Story and Music Sources

Story Sources and Notes

Six of the stories in the book are original tales by Peninnah Schram and Steven M. Rosman. Two of the stories are adaptations based on other sources.

"How to Sell a Menorah!" is based on a Moroccan story, "If You Give Me Money, I'll Give You a Hanukkiah" in *Aviteinu Sipru* (Hebrew), vol. 1, by Moshe Rabi. Jerusalem, Israel: Bakal Publishers, 1970. Israel Folktale Archives 8332.*

"The Secret of the Shammash" is based on an original story by Nissan Mindel, "The Tale of the Shammash" in *Talks and Tales*, ed. N. Mindel. Brooklyn, NY: Merkos L'Inyonei Chinuch, 1950. It appears by special permission. The episode with Elijah in the second half of this tale is based on Elijah variants. Also, in the second part of this tale, the motif of the riddles (IFA 11,459)* can be found in folktales such as "He Who Has Found a Wife,

151

Has Found a Great Good," collected by Kenny Shuler from Mazal Yakobi of Persia in *A Tale for Each Month 1976–1977* (Hebrew, Dov Noy). Haifa: IFA Publication Society, 1979.

The episodes in "A Melody in Israel" that deal with the rescue operation of immigrants from Italy to Israel are based on true historical events. The rescues at Bat Galim were described to Peninnah Schram several years ago by Ze'ev Hayam's daughter, Erella Hayam-Prihar, as they were walking near Bat Galim.

Note: The Israel Folktale Archives (IFA), founded by Dov Noy, has collected over 17,000 folktales in Israel. These tales are published in the IFA Publication Series, with over thirty-five volumes published by the Haifa Municipality Ethnological Museum and Folklore Archives. Each tale is classified according to its motif and assigned an IFA number.

Music Sources

CHANUKAH BLESSINGS

Traditional melody, ed. R. Neumann, from *Hanukah Melodies*. Cedarhurst, NY: Board of Jewish Education of Greater New York and Tara Publications, 1977.

Western Sephardi melody from *Sephardic Songs of Praise*, ed. A. L. Cardozo. Cedarhurst, NY: Tara Publications, 1987.

Original melody by Cantor S. E. Manchester from his book, *Kol Rinah Utfilah*, published by the composer, 1942.

HANEROT HALALU

Hasidic melody, arr. R. Neumann, from *Hanukah Melodies*. Cedarhurst, NY: Board of Jewish Education of Greater New York and Tara Publications, 1977.
Western Sephardi melody from *Sephardic Songs of Praise*, ed. A. L. Cardozo. Cedarhurst, NY: Tara Publications, 1987.

NIGGUN IN "THE PICTURE IN THE FLAME"

"Chanukah Nigun," arr. C. Davidson. Elkins Park, PA: Ashburne Music Publications, Inc., Division of Stonehedge, 1975.

MUSIC IN "A MELODY IN ISRAEL"

'Haneiros Halalu" (duet) by Cantor S. E. Manchester, in *Kol Rinah Utfilah*, published by the composer, 1942.
'Dovidl" (original title "Hershele"), by M. Gebirtig, in *Pearls of Yiddish Song*, compiled by E. G. Mlotek and J. Mlotek. New York: Education Department of the Workmen's Circle, 1988.
'Yam-Lid" (Song of the Sea), by M. Shneyer, Hebrew words by Judah ha-Levi, translated into Yiddish by C. N. Bialik. In *Pearls of Yiddish Song*. New York:

153

Education Department of the Workmen's Circle, 1988.

"Hatikvah" (The Hope). Jewish National Anthem. Melody with lyrics in Hebrew by N. H. Imber.

"Die Hoffenung" (The Hope). Yiddish translation by Cantor S. E. Manchester. In *Kol Rinah Utfilah*, 1942.

We have not included the Eastern Sephardi and Oriental melodies for the Chanukah blessings because there are no written musical notes for them. As the ritual of lighting candles in these cultures is so home-oriented, the families say the blessings with some kind of *nusach* or recitation that is improvised. Thus, there are no standard melodies for the blessings, except for the one in the Western Sephardi tradition that appears here. It is also interesting to note that the Eastern Sephardim do not say "shel Chanukah" at the end of the blessing, but simply "ner Chanukah."

Hanerot Halalu, a prayer that follows the candle blessing and recounts the miracle of Chanukah, is sung to an assortment of tunes and *niggunim*. We have included a very old chasidic melody. However, there are very few Sephardi melodies for this prayer.

An original composition for *Haneiros Halalu* by Cantor Samuel E. Manchester is included with the story "A Melody in Israel."

*Note: The music from *Sephardic Songs of Praise* is used by permission of Abraham Lopes Cardozo, editor, Tara Publications, Cedarhurst, NY. The music from *Kol Rinah Utfilah* by Cantor Samuel E. Manchester is used by permission of his daughter, Peninnah Schram.

Glossary

Antiochus–The tyrant who ruled the Syrian-Greek Empire during the time of the Maccabean revolt. He reached the throne in 175 B.C.E. and tried to bring all the people in his empire under the same religion. In his tyranny, he compelled the Jews to renounce their God and worship his pagan idols. In the small town of Modin, a local priest named Mattathias refused to pay homage to one of Antiochus's idols. Along with his five sons, who came to be called the Maccabees, Mattathias organized a revolt against Antiochus. Thus began the Maccabean revolt.

Ark–What holds the Torah scrolls in every synagogue sanctuary.

155

Badchan–Merrymaker or jester in Eastern Europe who entertained with song and rhyme at weddings and other festive occasions.

Bat Galim–A beach on the Mediterranean waterfront in Haifa. In Hebrew, literally "Daughter of the Waves."

Brenfire–Yiddish term referring to someone who is extremely lively and energetic; someone who stirs things up, like a "spitfire."

Bubbe–Yiddish for grandmother.

Bubbeleh–Diminutive form of grandmother. Literally, it means "little grandmother," but it is used as an affectionate term like "darling," "dear child," or "honey."

Cantor–Person who sings the liturgy in the synagogue. The cantor is called the *sheliach tzibur*, the messenger of the people, because s/he is responsible for chanting the prayers on their behalf. One of the requirements of a cantor is a sweet and clear voice.

Challah–Braided egg-bread eaten on Shabbat, Jewish holidays, and other special occasions. The plural is *challot* (Sephardi)/*challahs* (Ashkenazi).

Chanukah–In Hebrew, literally "dedication," and refers to that time in the year 165 B.C.E. when Judah and his army, called the Maccabees, defeated the army of the tyrant Antiochus IV Epiphanes and recaptured the holy Temple in Jerusalem. Antiochus's soldiers had defiled the Temple and established a center for the worship of Antiochus himself and other pagan idols. Judah and his brethren purified the Temple and rededicated it to the

156

service of God. The exploits of the Maccabees may be found in a variety of sources, from the Apocryphal Books of Maccabees 1 and 2, to Philo and the rabbis of the Talmud. The popular legend of the miraculous cruse of oil is actually attributed to the talmudic rabbis who lived centuries after the Maccabees.

Chanukiah-The special *menorah* or candelabra used specifically for Chanukah. It holds nine candles: one for each night of Chanukah and one for the *shammash*. The plural is *chanukiot*.

Chasidim-*See* rebbe.

Cheder-In Hebrew, literally "room," but it refers specifically to an old-fashioned elementary school for teaching Judaism. The same word is used in Yiddish.

Constantinople-Port in northwest Turkey built by Constantine I on the site of ancient Byzantium. Its name was changed to Istanbul in 1930.

Deportations-The transportation of Jews and others from their homes to the Nazi concentration and death camps.

Dreidle-Spinning top used during Chanukah. It has four sides, each displaying one of the four Hebrew letters: *nun*, *gimmel*, *hey*, and *shin*. These letters represent the Hebrew words: *Nes gadol hayah sham*, meaning "A great miracle happened there." The miracle refers to the cruse of oil found by the Maccabees when they won Jerusalem from the hands of Antiochus's armies. Thereupon they entered the holy Temple, which had been

157

defiled by Antiochus's troops. As they went about
cleansing the Temple, they discovered a small cruse that
seemed to hold just enough oil to burn for one night.
Miraculously, however, the oil burned for eight nights.
Hence, according to this tradition, we celebrate Chanukah for eight nights because of "the great miracle that
happened there."

Elijah the Prophet–In Hebrew, Eliyahu ha Navee.
Elijah is the most popular hero in Jewish folktales. A
prophet in Israel during the reigns of Ahab and Ahaziah
(ninth century B.C.E.), he is also associated with the
coming of the Messiah. As a character in folktales, Elijah
excels in miracles. Traditionally, he is associated with
Passover, but in folktales, he appears, usually in disguise,
throughout the year, performing miracles to help those
in need and to bring about justice.

Erev Chanukah–Literally, the "evening of Chanukah."
Since all Jewish holidays begin at sunset, *erev Chanukah*
refers to the first evening of Chanukah, or the very
beginning of the festival.

Gelt–The Yiddish word for "money." It is traditional to
give Chanukah *gelt* as a token gift, especially to children,
and to give Chanukah *gelt* for charity.

Graf–The Yiddish word for "nobleman." Anyone ele-
gantly dressed is referred to as "looking like a *graf*."

Haganah–The underground military organization of
the Jewish community in Israel, founded in 1920 after
the Arab riots. In World War II, many members of the
Haganah joined the British army. From the end of World

War II to 1948, the Haganah was very active in "illegal" immigration and anti-British activities. On May 31, 1948, Haganah became the regular army of Israel.

Haneiros (Haneirot) Halalu–The song a family sings after kindling the Chanukah lights and while watching the flames:

> We kindle these lights to commemorate the miracles and the wonders. These lights are sacred and we are not permitted to make use of them but are only supposed to admire them so as to give thanks and praise Your Name for Your miracles, Your wonders and Your deliverances.

Hayam, Ze'ev (1903–1977)–The name, which literally means "Wolf of the Sea," taken by Vladimir Yitskovitch after he immigrated to the land of Israel in 1924. Born in Odessa, he worked as a seaman on the Black Sea. Toward the end of the 1920s, he was certified in England as Captain, and when he returned to Israel, he enlisted in the British Navy and served as commander of all Israeli naval officers. He helped establish the principal sea routes to Israel and the school for marine officers. Before the establishment of the State of Israel, he was sent to Italy by the Haganah to purchase marine equipment for the rescue of Holocaust survivors to bring them to Israel. He directed many of the rescue operations at Bat Galim. After 1948, he was the main inspector of boats and ports in Israel for nineteen years, he wrote about the history of Hebrew shipping, and he established the Maritime Museum. His family now lives in Haifa.

Hershele Ostropolier (1757–1811) – Born in the Ukraine, this eighteenth-century jester/prankster lived in Miedziboz, Poland. Hershele was the jester to Rabbi Boruch of Miedziboz, one of the chasidic rebbes, who suffered from melancholia. Hershele was famous for his satiric barbs and his tales, and the stories and tales about him, which have made him a legendary character, have become part of Yiddish folklore and are widely told and enjoyed.

Inquisition–Here, the Spanish Inquisition, an institution established by the Catholic Church to combat heresy and enforce conversion to the Church. Its efforts climaxed with the expulsion of Jews from Spain in 1492.

Jewish Agency–First recognized in the British Mandate over Palestine, this organization, originally called the Jewish Affairs Department and renamed the Jewish Agency in 1929, acted as the unofficial government of the Jewish settlement until 1948 when many of its functions passed to the new Israeli government. It continued its responsibilities for immigration, absorption of new immigrants, and agricultural settlement. It now also has other activities, including education, outside of Israel.

Kislev–Name of the Hebrew month in which Chanukah falls. The 25th of Kislev is the first night of Chanukah.

Kugel–Yiddish word meaning "pudding." It usually refers to a pudding made either with potatoes or with noodles.

Landsleit–In Yiddish, people from the same country, "fellow countrymen."

Latke–A Yiddish word meaning "potato pancake," one of the traditional foods prepared by Eastern European Jews for Chanukah. In Israel one of the traditional Chanukah foods is a *soofganit*, which is a jelly doughnut. Both latkes and *soofganiyot* (plural of *soofganit*) are cooked in oil and, so, remind us of the oil found by the Maccabees, which burned miraculously for eight nights.

Maccabees–Name given to the heroes of Chanukah; namely, the sons of Mattathias and their followers. Mattathias had five sons: Judah, Yochanan, Eleazar, Jonathan, and Simon. The term maccabee usually is explained in one of these two ways. The name represents a transliteration of the Greek word for hammer and describes the manner in which Judah and his troops would launch a lightning strike upon Antiochus's troops. It also is believed to represent the first letters of the Hebrew expression translated as "Who is like you, O Lord, among the mighty?"

Maggid–A traveling preacher who teaches Torah through inspirational sermons and stories. Plural is *maggidim*.

Maoz Tzur–Thirteenth-century melody sung during Chanukah. Literally, "Rock of Ages."

Mazal–In Hebrew, "luck."

Megillah–Hebrew scroll. There are five scrolls (*megillot*) of biblical Hagiographa: Ruth, Song of Songs, Lamentations, Ecclesiastes, and Esther. The *megillah* of Esther is read on Purim and relates the story of Esther and Mordecai, who saved the Jews of the Persian Empire. The Megillah usually refers to the Book of Esther.

Menorah–*See chanukiah.*

161

Mezuzah-Hebrew for "doorpost." A *mezuzah* is a parchment scroll containing the name of God, enclosed in a decorative box and attached to the doorposts of rooms in a Jewish home. It is customary to kiss the *mezuzah* when entering or leaving a house.

Mi Y'maleil-Traditional Chanukah melody. Literally, "Who Can Retell."

Midrash-A method of interpreting scripture that teaches lessons through stories or homilies; a particular genre of rabbinic literature. A *midrash*, sometimes in the form of a story or folk tale, explains or "fills in the spaces between the words." Plural is *midrashim*.

Mitzvah-In Hebrew, "precept," "commandment," or "religious duty." Usually translated as a "good deed."

Mossad-Shortened form of Mossad L'Aliyah Bet, Hebrew for "Organization for Immigration B." This organization operated the unauthorized immigration beginning with the end of the Second World War in 1945 and continuing to statehood in 1948. The head of the Mossad was Shaul Avigur. The Mossad was responsible for bringing tens of thousands of homeless Jews to the Land of Israel. For an absorbing account of one of these enormous operations, read *Voyage to Freedom: An Episode in the Illegal Immigration to Palestine* by Ze'ev Venia Hadar and Ze'ev Tsahor (London, England, and Totowa, NJ: Vallentine, Mitchell and Company Limited, 1985).

Niggun-A chasidic melody or popular song, without words.

Nissim–Hebrew and Yiddish for "miracles." Plural of *nes*.

Nusach–Hebrew term with several meanings. Used here, it signifies a melodic pattern or prayer mode governing the traditional prayer texts. The melodies of prayers were informally passed on from generation to generation. In this manner, many melodies were collected into a body called *nusach*. Because it has no fixed rhythm or meter, this vehicle for prayer affords opportunity for improvisation. (For more information see Macy Nulman, *Concise Encyclopedia of Jewish Music*, New York: McGraw-Hill, 1975.)

Passover Seder–*Seder* is a Hebrew word meaning "order." The Passover Seder is the ceremony held on the first night of Passover (and in many communities on the second night, as well) during which the story of the Exodus of the Hebrews from Egypt is recounted. The special book used to conduct the seder is called a *Haggadah*.

Peretz, Yehuda Leib–Peretz (1852–1915) is one of the three fathers of Yiddish literature, along with Mendele Mocher Sforim and Sholom Aleichem. Many of his stories are well-known, often drawn from Jewish folklore and chasidic literature for inspiration.

Persia–Official name of Iran before 1935.

Rabbi Akiva–One of the greatest rabbis of the late first and early second centuries. During the Bar Kochba revolt against Rome in 132 B.C.E., Akiva continued to teach Torah to his students despite Roman edicts prohibiting such activities. Eventually, Akiva was captured

163

and imprisoned by the Romans. Yet, even in the midst of torture, Akiva continued to teach Torah. His name has become synonymous with scholarship and courage.

Rachamim–Hebrew and Yiddish for "mercy."

Rashi–Acronym for Rabbi Shelomo Yitzhaki. This eleventh-century French scholar is considered the greatest of all Jewish biblical commentators.

Rebbe–Yiddish word meaning "my teacher," and used to refer to the spiritual leader of a chasidic community. The modern chasidim trace their ancestry back to an eighteenth-century mystical, saintly storyteller named Israel ben Eliezer (later known as the Baal Shem Tov or "The Master of the Good Name"). Early Chasidism was known for its rejection of formal rabbinical learning and teaching in favor of a simple, joyous kind of worship often characterized by *niggunim*, rapturous dancing, and parables. Each group of chasidim had its own rebbe, who commanded great loyalty and singular respect.

Shabbat (Sephardi), **Shabbos** (Ashkenazi)–Hebrew word for Sabbath. The Jewish Sabbath begins at sunset on Friday and continues to sunset on Saturday.

Shadchente–Yiddish word for a female matchmaker. A male matchmaker is *shadchen*.

Shammash–The ninth candle used to kindle each of the other Chanukah candles as they are lit on each of the eight nights of Chanukah. No other candle can be used for the purpose of kindling the others. (Sometimes referred to as *shammas*.)

Shehecheyanu–In Hebrew, literally "Who has kept us in life." This prayer, or *b'rachah*, of thanksgiving is recited on the first day of Chanukah at the end of the two candle blessings. It is also recited at certain other holidays and at happy occasions of celebration, such as weddings, *bar* and *bat mitzvahs*, births, etc.

> We praise You, Lord our God, King of the Universe, Who has kept us in life, sustained us and enabled us to reach this occasion.

Shtetl–Yiddish word meaning "a little city," or "village." In some *shtetlach* (plural of *shtetl*) of Galicia, Lithuania, Poland, the Ukraine, Romania, Hungary, Bessarabia, and Bohemia, the inhabitants were poor folk and mostly Jews. In other *shtetlach*, they were all Jews.

Shtibl–Yiddish word meaning "little house." It refers to small houses of prayer, especially among the chasidim.

Shul–In Yiddish, "synagogue."

Song of Songs–The composition of this most beautiful love poem, one of the Five *Megillot* (Scrolls), is credited to King Solomon. It is traditionally read on Passover and by Sephardi Jews on Sabbath. *See also megillah.*

Tiere–Yiddish term of affection meaning "dear."

Torah–Hebrew handwritten scroll that contains the first five books of the Hebrew Bible: Genesis, Exodus, Leviticus, Numbers, and Deuteronomy. (In Hebrew these are: Bereshit, Shemot, Vayikra, Bamidbar, and Devarim.) It

is the holiest of all Jewish ritual objects and is housed in the Ark.

Tzedakah-Hebrew word meaning "justice" or "righteousness"; more specifically, refers to deeds performed in the interest of justice and righteousness. Although commonly used to mean charity, it encompasses much more. Jewish tradition teaches that *tzedakah* is one of the pillars upon which our world rests.

Yarmulke-Skull cap.

Yavo-Common term meaning "come in," in response to a knock on the door. In Hebrew, literally "He who will come."

Yom tov-In Hebrew, a festival or holy day. Used in Yiddish too, but pronounced *Yontuf*.

Zaide-Yiddish for grandfather.